SHERLOCK HOLMES AND
THE MENACING MELBOURNIAN

- global intrigue set against a background of distant war as
Holmes and Watson confront a desperate and determined
colonial with his mind set on establishing
a new empire of crime.

Allan Mitchell

Paperback ISBN 978-1-78092-965-1
ePub ISBN 978-1-78092-966-8
PDF ISBN 978-1-78092-967-5

Published in the UK by MX Publishing
335 Princess Park Manor, Royal Drive,
London, N11 3GX www.mxpublishing.co.uk

Cover design by Brian Belanger

INTRODUCTION

When Arthur Conan Doyle took up his pen in favour of an underused stethoscope, he could scarcely have imagined that his story of an infuriatingly inspired and intrepid detective with a school-boy sense of justice and questionable social skills would hold the imaginations of generations across the world and become both the first and last word in the science of reasoned deduction. That detective, the ever-famous Sherlock Holmes, has had his imitators but none has ever come close to challenging Sherlock's supremacy in intuitive and instinctive insight into the criminal mind. This, only Sherlock can claim and, coupled with his hard-won knowledge of every devious crime and felonious outrage committed in and before his time, as well as the drive and energy to pursue the hidden truth, it gives the Great Sleuth, and him alone, the right to the title of The Greatest Detective Who Ever Lived.

Sherlock emerged from a civilisation rapidly taking itself into uncharted territory – new understanding of the workings of the world and, indeed, the universe was coupled with great technological advances. Steam power, electrical energy, rapid communication, to name just a few – all undergoing revolutionary change and each leapfrogging the other as advances in one field fed into those of others. The beast, however, was still in us – the pack instinct was still there – it just had new and more deadly ways of expressing itself. Individuals, cities and nations were advised, as a famous statesman of the period declared, to 'speak softly and carry a big stick'. The speech, however, had been getting harsher and the sticks had grown even bigger.

It was well before the black and white antics of a cartooned newspaper detective gave us the square-jawed 'Dick' chasing down felons between the skyscrapers of New York that a pipe-smoking contemplative 'Sherlock' used brain over brawn to out-think and out-smart the forces of evil, evil which had festered on the poorly-lit, smoky and dangerous streets of London. Both epithets endure, 'Dick' summoning up images of a tough-talking, hard-drinking, chain-smoking police detective barking out orders through his intercom or, perhaps, of a private investigator operating with the assistance of a platinum-blonde phone-answering dictation-taking secretary in possession of a mother complex and infinite patience while helping out with jobs which no one else would touch with a barge pole. On the other hand, 'Sherlock' is applied to anyone showing formerly unsuspected super-human powers of insight and deduction while also being somewhat socially inept. Conversely, 'Sherlock' could be a term of derision used sarcastically about any mere mortal discovering and announcing the glaringly obvious.

Both Dick and Sherlock have earned their places in the imaginations of millions but, while Dick will readily use a tyre-screeching squad car and a .38 to force his way to the truth, Sherlock arrives sedately in a Hansom cab to deftly sweep away layer upon layer of falsehood with a fine mental brush to reveal the hidden facts of the matter at hand, though a single stick applied across the knuckles or bridge of the nose may, at times, be necessary to speed things along.

With the square-jawed Dick, however, the reader is rarely taken along to participate in the mental machinations of bringing the criminal perpetrators to justice, one is merely shown what happens when enough force is applied to counter that of the wrong-doers. While officialdom has no choice but to act, Sherlock can pick and choose both the case and its manner of investigation as well as his degree of interaction with the bureaucratic machinery of Justice. More than once has Sherlock exercised discretion and maintained his silence when he has felt Justice to be sufficiently served in its natural sense while overlooking the overly-strict tenets of Law. Sherlock has rules and respects the Law in principle but knows well that Law is often a poor servant of Justice.

Above all, though, it is the Chase for which Sherlock yearns, much less so than the Kill for which he often loses interest. Sherlock will always be there, the Hound hard on the heels of its Quarry with Watson sitting square in the saddle and sounding the Charge in yet another case challenging the wits and intellect of the Greatest of Sleuths. We do not have to look far to find Sherlock, he exists in every form of media we have contrived – he is alive and will live on forever in the minds of the imaginative.

CONTENTS

SHERLOCK HOLMES AND THE MENACING MELBOURNIAN

THE MESSAGE

Sherlock Holmes had been instrumental in defusing a plot designed to usher in a world-shattering catastrophe which Colonel Moran, one-time right-hand man to the professorial evil arch-fiend Moriarty, had brought to the brink of execution. Nations already suspicious of each others' motives had been put on alert and were heading toward a war footing by actions put into play, albeit in a clumsy and inept fashion, by Moran.

The plan, originally devised by Moriarty but never implemented due to his disappearance at the Reichenbach Falls, required that the major European powers be pushed into war with each other and that substantial quantities of Britain's gold reserves be intercepted and hidden offshore while being moved for security reasons. As Europe became embattled to the point of exhaustion, a new dictator would emerge to take control as the virtual ruler of all Europe and, by extension, the world. The plan was fatally flawed and never seriously considered by Moriarty. To have the remotest chance of success, it would have required the finesse of someone with the incredibly immense intellect of the Great Fiend, something which Moran, as cunning and ruthless as he was, could never hope to claim.

The nations of Europe had been approaching armed conflict as a result of false documents fed maliciously to their London embassies but, alerted by a body of concerned citizens well-placed to notice developments affecting the City and Realm and nicknamed the Knights of the Tower of London, Whitehall was able to nip such developments in the bud. It then only remained to catch the plotters in the act of carrying out the large-scale theft of bullion, bullion which was in fact Lead painted to resemble Gold. Whitehall, Scotland Yard, numerous Police units, the Army and Navy were joined by Holmes and Watson in the plan to capture those who had brought menace to the Great Metropolis and, indeed, the entire World. A visit by Holmes and Watson to Mycroft in anticipation of celebrations and pleasant conversation came abruptly to a halt on Mycroft's surprise comment on a recently delivered note declaring peace but signed simply with 'M' ...

"The initial's correct, Brother Mine, I agree,
But whoever had sent you that note wasn't me."

Shocked and not knowing exactly what to think, apart from that which his mind did not wish to contemplate, Sherlock Holmes turned to his brother and said ...

"Brother Mycroft, don't tell me it wasn't your note
And that 'M' wasn't yours but from someone who wrote
With a view to tormenting my mind in a way
That would give it no rest, not for even one day."

"If the M's not for Mycroft, then who could it be
Than someone whose initial would unsettle me
But who must be presumed to have died in that blast
Off the coast when he saw he'd been beaten at last."

"It was not Moriarty – he's long dead and gone
Though Moran tried to capture the light that had shone
On his evil empire, now shattered, destroyed,
Although some of his tactics, the man has employed."

"But I cannot conceive how the boat for the Gold
Was destroyed out at sea by a person so cold
And corrupt unless he, himself, set off the fuse
To the bomb for, to submit, he'd surely refuse."

"I must give this some thought – could it possibly be
That there might have been more to that catastrophe?
How could one have expected the boat to explode
When confronted in sight of Moran's mother lode?"

"One just wouldn't have time to construct the device
Or could pay one enough to make that sacrifice.
The bomb was on board, primed before the boat sailed,
I'd presume, just in case the foul enterprise failed."

"What must now be considered? What can we expect?
What part of a plan have we yet to detect?
Come, Watson, we must, to our diggings, repair -
There's tobacco to burn – I've had too much fresh air."

Back at Baker Street, Holmes, in a dense cloud of smoke,
Would consider the facts, but he finally spoke
After hours of silence, *"Watson, I would say*
Someone needed Moran to be out of the way."

"That Percy, now captured, had been on the ground
And directing the movements of gang members bound
For the dockyards of Grimsby, the railway yards,
Although we held the aces in that game of cards."

"Could it be, and it's more than a fanciful fact,
That Moran was at sea and about to contact
His lieutenant to transfer the gold to the boat
Upon docking, all ready to swagger and gloat?"

"So, was there another, to us still a stranger,
Suspecting a trick, recognising the danger
And having resources and sufficient daring
To blow up the boat and its crew without caring?"

"That man would have needed, some time in advance,
To set up a device which would not have a chance
Of exploding unless everything went awry -
It would blow if the Navy was getting close by."

"The great blast, I believe, if I'm not off the mark,
Could have been set off by an electrical spark
When some prearranged act by the Captain would close
Some electrical circuit when problems arose."

"What that act might have been, I'm unable to say
For the blast would have blown any clues far away.
And, of course, things all sank into water quite deep
And the sea, as you know, all its secrets, will keep."

"The Navy had searched, though nobody was found,
Unsurprisingly, living and floating around
In the flotsam left after the deed had been done -
No survivors were picked up, not one single one."

"And no dead were collected – it seems they all went
To the bottom with Moran who also was sent
To a place where no marker could show where he fell.
For a monster like him, I think that's just as well."

"My conjecture is that someone else, not Moran,
Had been calling the shots or outwitted the man
Into thinking that he was in charge of the plot
But intended to dupe him the first chance he got."

"But, if that might have been, it is possible, too,
That whoever that was - call him 'M', that will do
For the moment at least – saw through our counter plan
And then sacrificed all, everyone to a man."

"This M would have been ready, if things went awry,
To escape all suspicion by being quite sly
And awaiting the boat, or news of its destruction,
In Belgium or Holland – that is my deduction."

Watson, ever so puzzled, broke in on his friend
Saying' *"Well, My Good Fellow, I surely commend*
All your thoughts on the matter, although I'm confused
On the way that the Captain was callously used."

"How could 'M' be so sure that the Captain would blow
Up his boat right on cue? Just how could this 'M' know
That the Captain would act in the way that he ought -
The way that the one we call 'M' would have sought?"

Holmes responded with, *"Ah! And it's only a guess,*
But the Captain could claim lack of knowledge unless
He had documents with him, instructions and maps,
To be jettisoned if intercepted, perhaps."

"I'd think they'd be held in a strongbox which could
Be picked up and thrown overboard rapidly should
They be ordered to halt by the Naval Command –
Any proof would be gone – they'd be so far from land."

"I would say as that box would be lifted, a wire
Attached to a switch would pull hard and would fire
A detonator which would set off the charge
Of explosive material, ever so large."

"I guess that the Captain would have been forbidden
To move such a box from where it had been hidden
Unless intercepted – his only recourse
Would be throw the box overboard - quickly, of course."

"But, if things went to plan, perhaps Percy would sever
That wire in secret – the Captain would never
Know of the great danger in which he had been -
To risk being blown up, he wouldn't be keen."

"Perhaps there was a key Percy had to supply
Upon loading the Gold - and this would explain why
The boat's Captain had never been tempted to glance
At his future instructions – no key, so no chance."

"I feel, all along, even Percy the Ponce
Would be wary enough of Moran to ensconce
Himself in with this 'M' - he's a weasel and sly
But a seasoned survivor – he's slimy and spry."

"Unless Percy will talk, of course, we'll never know
If our reasoned conjecture will help us to show
That this M, the thirteenth of our letters, has been
Quite unlucky so far, though he hasn't been seen."

"Well, he may have been seen and perhaps he is close."
Declared Watson, now feeling a little morose.
"And his agents may well have been watching us all -
He may not be in Belgium, but home in Pall Mall."

Sherlock heard Watson speak but took time to reply
For he'd little to go on but needed to try
To keep fact and conjecture apart until he
Could decide what the next move to make ought to be.

"That is certainly possible, Watson, My Friend.
We have little to go on except, at the end
Of our little adventure, a message was sent
From the one we call 'M' – we shall need a fresh scent."

"The hounds are now resting - the hunt wore them out."
Replied Watson, *"A few may be out and about*
But the bulk of the pack will be home fast asleep
And we may well be bitten if we make a peep."

"I do feel we have time to come up with a plan
With the help of Mycroft to uncover the man
Who we know just as 'M', for now stripped of his power;
Perhaps we could seek the advice of The Tower."

"That is what we shall do, My Dear Friend, I'll advise
Dr Denton that we need some words from the wise."
Uttered Sherlock, aware that must now accept
Watson's input – a promise that, so far, he'd kept.

Sherlock scribbled a note to be speedily taken
And given to Denton so he could awaken
The Tower of London and get it to meet
At the usual place on the usual street.

"In the meantime, John Watson, revisit your haunts
As though you were on one of your afternoon jaunts.
Talk about anything but do not mention Gold -
Gather news, My Good Doctor, be that new or old."

"What is said, what is not – it is all to be noted;
Also what is hinted and openly quoted.
If it's human, it will want to say to someone
What it knows of events and what soon will be done."

"We are quite funny creatures, Watson, you must know
And we are, by our nature, too eager to show
That we are up to date, we just love riddles deep
And a secret's a thing which most people can't keep."

"But, Watson, you need to go home to your wife
Before she comes looking for you with a knife
Or for me, for that matter – so go, don't delay."
But Watson said, *"Holmes, she'll just send me away."*

"Well, just give her the chance and give her my regards
But don't tell her of chases through dark railway yards
And of massive explosions and Captains that drown -
Take your wife out to dinner and show her the town."

Watson said *"That will make her suspicious, you know,*
And she may well ask questions – I hope I won't show
Her that I still have fears for the weeks right ahead -
Can't I send her a big bunch of flowers instead?"

"Get away with you, Watson – you've just taken on
The worst scum in the country and leapt right upon
Some despicable characters making them yield -
When you talk to your wife, you will not need a shield."

"Well, her words can be cutting, incredibly sharp,
Or the sounds which an angel might make with a harp.
There's just no way to know." declared Watson, afraid,
"The Devil himself sometimes has to be paid."

"Well, we've seen off the Devil and some of his beasts
And we've had one or two quite inedible feasts
While out chasing his demons," said Sherlock, amused,
"But of any great evil, your wife's not accused."

"You'll not need your revolver, nor cover of dark;
You're not out on those moorlands, so dreary and stark.
So go, My Good Friend, to your home and your Mary -
She's a wonderful woman and not very scary."

So, home, Watson shuffled, a little confused
At the way Sherlock pushed him away – had he used
Up his time as a partner-in-full and was now
Relegated to domestic duties, somehow?

Or, had Sherlock discovered compassion within
That magnificent mind, for he did have a grin
On his face saying Watson had nothing to fear -
On the facts of this matter, he wasn't too clear.

He would not take a Hansom, he wanted to walk
And to think what to say when he got home to talk
About what he'd been doing, the things he had seen,
Though, to give all the details, he wouldn't be keen.

Upon reaching his house, Watson found that the door
Was unlatched and ajar and inside, on the floor,
Was a brand new valise and a new walking stick -
Was his Mary applying the honey on thick?

Or was this Mary saying, *"Goodbye – you should go."*?
Inside, he must enter to learn *"Yes"* or *"No"*.
So he stood quite erect, took a breath good and deep,
And he stepped right on in for the man wouldn't creep.

Inside there was light and a table was set
Full of indulgent treats and, also, better yet,
There was Mary, all smiles, pouring wine in a glass -
It seems his reception was truly first-class.

"Welcome back from your battles. I've just had a note
Saying I should expect you. It says, and I quote,
'Your illustrious husband is now on his way -
I suppose I can spare him, at least for one day.'."

"Now, who do you think might have sent that to me?
There is only one person the sender could be.
It was Sherlock - it seems that the man wants to show
The respect you deserve." Mary said, all aglow.

"I had thought that your old valise looked a bit drab
So I bought you a new one and then thought to grab
A magnificent walking stick which you can swing -
You can't go chasing blaggards without such a thing."

Watson sat, flabbergasted and really quite lost
For appropriate words; he expected that frost
Might accompany those he'd receive from his wife
But it seemed she'd accepted his turbulent life.

"My Dear," he exclaimed, *"it's too much to expect*
From a dutiful wife, but do I now detect
A desire to have me at home for a day,
Perhaps two, before Sherlock Holmes drags me away?"

She replied, *"Of your exploits, I don't wish to hear*
For I know there was danger, that's perfectly clear.
But for better or worse was the vow that I made,
And the best is a thing I just never would trade."

THE WALK

In the meantime, a message, Sherlock had despatched
To find Denton, the Doctor, to say there was hatched
A new possible threat, though it might not amount
To much more than a bluff of a quite small account.

Denton swung into action and rapidly wrote
Out, to all in the Tower, a summoning note
To gather at Andre's restaurant that Thursday
To determine if anything might be in play.

It was Tuesday, already, so notice was short,
But all those in the Tower would jump to support
Any call for assistance if bodily able -
In the meantime, The Chef would prepare a fine table.

Of course, Watson received the same note with a look
That his wife, in an instant, instinctively took
As a call out to arms which her husband would heed
Like a grand knight of old going off on his steed.

But for just a few hours, perhaps a few days,
John Watson was hers and would bend to her ways
Till he took up his shield and lance and departed
For battle with forces in places uncharted.

"I won't ask," she declared *"what that note had to say
But I fear that, quite soon, you must be on your way."*
"That's not so," he replied, *"I have people to meet
But, for two days, it seems I'll be under your feet."*

"I'll take what there is," Mary stated to John,
*"And, for two days or ten, you'll be waited upon
Like the Lord of some Manor with servants aplenty -
I suppose Sherlock couldn't extend it to twenty."*

"Twenty days of such pampering and I'd not be
Any use to myself or to Sherlock, as we
Need to be fairly fit for the risks we must take."
John replied, *"But I will have a large slice of cake."*

Although home, Watson went on an extended walk
On both days, seeing people and making small-talk
About subjects diverse, seeking gossip and tale
About anything happening on any scale.

He knew well that a smidgin of rumour could hold
The first hint of some trouble about to unfold
Although not, in itself, of a threatening tone -
This must all be collated, not mulled on alone.

He would keep all facts separate until he had met
With the rest of the Tower, at which time he'd get
Every chance to divulge any strange bit of news
And discuss, with the others, their divergent views.

All the rest would do likewise, they all knew the drill;
It would be unproductive, extremely, to spill
Any unguarded word which felons might detect
As a hint that, their knowledge, they ought to protect.

So, he went to the markets, examining fruit
On the barrows, displayed; he checked out a new suit
At his tailors while, all the time, listening hard
For the barest of hints – his own words he would guard.

He would speak with the cabbies and ask them the best
Way to get across London, and then take a rest
At a coffee-shop offering beverage and bun
Acting like a buffoon, new in town, having fun.

He would get people talking on subjects diverse
Taking care not to generate comment adverse;
Many facts he would gather, though none to alarm
Him by sounding as though there was impending harm.

All that day he roamed London's streets seemingly lost,
Drinking far too much coffee which would, to his cost,
Keep him wide awake through many hours of night -
Next day he'd be mindful of that sleepless plight.

Back to hearth and to home, Watson slowly progressed
Somewhat tired, of course, and not fully impressed
With his outing's results, though it may well emerge
It might prove otherwise when the knights all converge.

"That was quite a good walk you have taken, My Dear."
Declared Mary as she saw her husband appear
On the stairs of their house, *"But tomorrow please rest
So, when you're at your meeting, you'll be at your best."*

"Just an hour or so," replied Watson, *"I'll take
In the morning - that exercise surely will make
All the difference, that is if I have a short sleep
After noon, just as long as it isn't too deep."*

Next morning he breakfasted then he set out
On his quest around London, first giving a shout
Telling Mary he's leaving and would be back soon,
But definitely it would be before noon.

He went back to the markets, inspected the wares
On display while he stated that *"Nothing compares
To the produce of Britain."* expecting reproach
Which would help him, appropriate subjects, to broach.

"The produce of Britain – well, that is a giggle.
There are very few places bananas could wiggle
Their ways from a tree to this box anywhere
But the tropics." the stallholder stated, *"So there!"*

"And my dates," said his partner, *"I'm certain, will not*
Grow in Britain unless it's a hothouse you've got.
Even then there isn't much chance you'll succeed -
I'll give you the produce of Britain, indeed."

"You'll be telling me next that we mine all our Gold
Down in Kent or up north near the Clyde where it's cold.
It's Australia and Africa sending Gold forth,
California too, and Alaska up north."

Watson thought to himself, *"That's an odd thing to say.*
I was speaking of food then the man made his way
Off the track telling me of where Gold has been mined.
Would the fellow, to tell me some more, be inclined."

"Gold," replied Watson, *"is just where you find it.*
Somebody once said. I, for one, wouldn't mind it
If I could find some in my garden out back -
I would dig the stuff up and put it in a sack."

"It's not the Gold miners who come back all rich
With their pockets all bulging, it's other types which
Get the fools with pickaxes and shovels to dig."
Said the fig seller, softly, *"They can make it big."*

"There are men, I have heard, who opted to remain
In South Africa, willingly, hoping to gain
Some advantage with all of the land in turmoil -
They are not staying on to farm Africa's soil."

"No, indeed?" queried Watson, *"The war's almost won*
And I thought every man, every fine British son
Would return to his home, to his barracks at least.
The African climate, I'm told, is a beast."

"Just don't you believe it." the fig seller stated,
"Temptation and greed will have many fixated
And very prepared to, their comforts, forego
In the quest for an African El-Dorado."

"Why! My very own cousin went off for a year
And returned with a tale of a man in his ear
Who was once in the Army till better things beckoned -
A Colonial officer, that's what he reckoned."

"Those Irregulars, see, had the Boers on the run
As the fellows, like Boers, had been born to the gun
And the horse and the land, and they knew how to beat
The old Boer at his game – that was no easy feat."

"But he says - that's my cousin - that officer had,
In his youth, been a bit of a tear-away lad
And had grown up in Melbourne, right deep in the city,
He showed little fear and, at times, little pity."

"That is hard to believe," countered Watson, all ears
For the fig seller's tale, *"It's a land full of tears*
For the lives that were lost. Is your cousin so sure
That the land of South Africa's one to endure."

"You can get used to anything, so I am told,
If there is the promise of riches in Gold
To be picked from the pockets of miners, unwary -
Some men will try anything, however scary."

21

Watson knew that he mustn't put questions, direct,
He must sound flabbergasted and prone to reject
The suggestion that officers could be corrupt -
He'd goad the fig seller hoping he'd interrupt.

"That an officer under the banners of She,
Our good Queen, most beloved, could ever so be
That devoid of all principle boggles my mind -
I suppose, though, the man's a Colonial kind."

"He's a brave man, Jack tells us, as brave as can be."
Said the chatty fig seller, *"Much braver than we*
Could expect of our soldiers – perhaps he is mad
But perhaps a good leader gone totally bad."

"He's a tiger in battle, well, that's what Jack tells.
Jack, my cousin, that is - the man slashes and yells
Till the enemy's dead or retreated away.
Men fear and respect him, well, that's what they say."

"Brevet Major – that's right." the fig seller exclaimed.
"Someone raised up in office till peace was proclaimed
When he'd have to revert to his earlier rank.
That wouldn't go well with a man of such swank."

"It's coming back to me. The man, so they say -
Well, my cousin who'd know it – had sailed away
Out of Melbourne, Victoria, off to the fight -
A militia Lieutenant, if I've got it right."

Watson tried to feign interest of general degree
But he felt his heart thumping - his mind was set free
With the thought that there might be a clue to be had
From this officer, once a colonial lad.

"A tiger, you say. Well, perhaps that's his name.
But, if that is his title, no one would be game
To presume to address him by that accolade -
What would the men call when out on parade?"

"I just cannot recall," the fig seller replied,
"But he had a nickname which was often applied,
Rarely straight to his face, mostly behind his back -
Oh yes. Mick, that is, Michael - the lads called him Mack."

Watson gave a short *"Hrrmff"* and an indistinct *"Mack"*
And he thought it was time to retreat, not attack,
So he said, *"I'll have dates - and bananas, as well -*
That's an interesting story your cousin can tell."

"I will take these back home as a treat for the wife
And I'll tell her it's grown, with an absence of strife,
In the South Downs of Sussex – she'll know it's a tease
But she'll just play along - I'm quite easy to please."

"A treat for the Missus, well isn't that dandy;
In the stall, two along, there's a man making candy
And lollies of all sorts – but, Boy, can he brag."
Said the fig seller, placing the figs in a bag.

"Now I remember." the fig seller shouted,
"That Mack who had, all of the rules of war, flouted
Was called McIntyre – sounds Irish to me -
But, no matter, the man is as wild as can be."

Watson gave a *"Thank you!"* and thought, with a smile,
"I gave him an inch, he returned me a mile
Of what might be of interest, although maybe not,
But at least, for the Tower, there's something I've got."

He continued his walk but he just couldn't get
Off his mind that he had, by not asking more, let
A fine opportunity slip through his fingers -
He knew that was wrong but a thought like that lingers.

"I should go home right now and make notes for tonight.
I must not think too much lest my fancy take flight
And embellish those things which the fig seller told
About soldiers and Boers and South African Gold."

With his figs and bananas and packet of candy,
Watson took a short-cut which he knew to be handy;
He felt his flesh creep as he tried not to mull
Over facts in his mind – at least life wasn't dull.

"This seems to go on, this affair of the Gold."
He would muse to himself, quite forgetting the hold
That it had on so many – the promise it gave
To a prince or a pauper, a magnate or knave.

"Perhaps we will hear, as Knights of the Round Table,
If those of the Tower are possibly able
To shed any light on this lingering plot,
If that's what it is – it's a quite gnarly knot."

Watson walked at a pace, slow but steady, and found
That, by thinking of dinner, his mind had unwound
And released all the tension he'd started to feel -
Against any more trouble, his mind he would steel.

At his doorstep, he halted – made certain he'd not
Give away, to his wife, any hint of a plot
Which might be under way – so he took a deep breath -
There was no way he'd frighten his wife half to death.

His wife was of sterner stuff than he suspected;
The instant she saw him come in, she detected
A change in demeanour but, too, kept her head -
She would not let him see she had feelings of dread.

"*Ah! Some goodies for me!*" she declared with delight
As her husband came in and she gazed on the sight
Of a bag of bananas and dates and of candy -
"*After lunch, I believe, they will all come in handy.*"

After lunch, Watson said he would have a good rest
So tonight, at the dinner, he'd be at his best;
He regretted he couldn't take Mary along
But to give her the smallest of hints would be wrong.

As he mounted the stairs to his bedroom he mused
On the wayward colonial standing accused
Of behaviour a great deal less than the norm
He'd expect by those wearing the Queen's uniform.

But rest would evade him, though try as he may
To get just a few hours of sleep in the day;
His mind was alert and was racing with thought
Even though, not to turn to conjecture, he ought.

He would toss and then turn, punch his pillow so it
Would, with such brutal treatment, give in and submit
To caressing his head until each unsettled notion
Was gone and his mind had been freed of commotion.

But, alas, though he tried, Watson couldn't relax
As the thoughts went around in a way which would tax
Any mind holding scruples of average extent -
John Watson's fine mind, any rest, would prevent.

He lay there, despondent, aware that the facts
Were all that he should tell – speculation detracts
From objective assessment – he knew this too well
His imaginings, though, had proved too hard to quell.

So he rose and he dressed, read the paper some more
Attempting to empty his mind of its store
Of imaginings dreadful and beyond belief -
To get going that evening would be a relief.

He would walk to a pre-arranged spot where he'd meet
Up with Holmes and then wait until, into the street,
The four-wheeler of Richards would turn right on time
Taking them, and the others, to dinner sublime.

Mrs Tully they picked up, but Lady Devine
Had sent word on ahead that she'd definitely dine
But might be a tad late for her husband was leaving
That evening for something that had his chest heaving.

The usual banter was filling the carriage -
Talk of the Queen's health and the possible marriage
Of some remote princess to some unknown prince -
Sherlock Holmes, at this trivial small talk would wince.

But, in time, they would enter the lane, as before,
And proceed to the restaurant holding, in store,
Expectations of dinner and, then, conversation
On anything posing a threat to the nation.

THE VELDT

A war, there had been, for some time, raging hot
Over Africa's Veldt after there'd been a plot
By some locals to form a new nation apart
From the Empire which Britain drew on the world chart.

There'd been movements of people of differing hue
Both from Europe and Africa who would subdue
Territory and the people who lived on the land
As the south tracts of Africa came in demand.

There had been an uprising two decades before
When the local Boer settlers dissented and swore
That they'd run their own show, form a nation apart -
Britain let them self-govern by Treaty - quite smart.

But not smart enough for Transvaal began filling
With strangers whose numbers were constantly spilling
Out onto the lands seeking out all its wealth -
To the Boers, it would seem this was conquest by stealth.

The Transvaal would be theirs and it did come to be
They'd again take up arms and tell Britain that she
Ought to honour her Treaty, keep strangers away -
But the flow was unstoppable – they'd come to stay.

So fight, the Boers did, in their own special way
Which meant not marching out in a gaudy display
But by skirmishing often – surprise was supreme -
They might just drive a wedge in the Empire's scheme.

But a call then went out for the Empire to fight
The Boer farmers' militias with all of the might
Which could be brought to bear so that Africa's spine
Could be charted in bright British red down its line.

'Cape to Cairo', the catch-cry, for Empire builders
For trade now transacted in Pounds, not in Guilders
Nor Pieces-of-Eight, at each venerable club
In London, the city, the world's vibrant hub.

Africa, to so many, presented the prize,
The arena of commerce of such a great size
And of massive return that all effort was made
To expand the Empire, its demise evade.

There were benefits, true, which the land might receive
Such as trade, education - but some would perceive
Opportunity, great, for their personal gain -
Gold and Diamonds littered the land, clear and plain.

"Throw more men at the enemy, don't let us down."
Was the cry which was made to those close to the Crown
With no thought of the blood being spilled every day
From the men who would die, from their homes, far away.

In time, the Boers found they must be overtaken
By forces, unstoppable – great dreams forsaken
Despite a defence, never short of heroic,
An outlook, determined, decidedly stoic.

In war's aftermath, victors covet the spoils;
Adventurers see how the massive turmoils
Favour bold and unscrupulous men once released
From their units as discipline actively ceased.

Addicted to action, alone and in bands,
Some would ravage whatever was left on the land
Taking items of value, though pickings are slim
After long years of warfare, horrific and grim.

A few would succeed, most would just disappear
From the face of the Earth and all that they'd held dear
As they would, town-to-town, on the new frontiers, stray
And the meanness of life took all prospects away.

Some were bitter, extremely, for once they had been
Sent to battle for glory, for their noble Queen;
Their comrades had died in their thousands for land
Far away from their homes for the Empire grand.

'Soldiers of the Queen' was the song they all knew -
It was sung on the march with the Boer in full view;
It was they who had conquered and they who prevailed
But their units were recalled – their glory had sailed.

Was there someone to follow, somebody to lead
Them to battle and glory, somebody to read
Them their orders again in a manner inspired?
Such a leader and life was all that they desired.

Well, there was one to do it, an officer who
Recognised that a war offered great prospects to
Anyone who could fight but not care who might win -
Independent and mobile, he'd plot from within.

He had fought with irregular troops for a time
In the wars with the Zulus, discovering crime
Often went hand-in-hand with the skills he acquired -
War gave to the fellow just what he desired.

McIntyre had found what he truly loved best
Was the fight in a drawn-out and bloody contest
And became, on the Veldt, a notorious man -
It was there that the fellow met Colonel Moran.

From India, Moran was on-loan, in a sense,
For the Indian Army went to the expense
Of transferring him off to the African sphere -
An advisor, it said, though it wasn't sincere.

He was rather too much the adventurer sort -
'Reckless courage' it read in a recent report
Which most read as 'undisciplined', likely as not -
He was quite the loose cannon when things got too hot.

McIntyre was like him but came from the streets
Where, with smoke, an enduring uncertainty greets
One each morning, though he showed a definite flair
For ascending to heights to breathe much cleaner air.

He had grown up in Melbourne, a Saint Kilda boy,
And the toughs of the suburbs knew well not to toy
With this wild Melbourne lad, but a brush with the Law
Saw him off with the Colours – escape, the lad saw.

Colonial Victoria was keen to display
A mature disposition and send on its way,
To the African battles, detachments of red -
He would be in his element where-ever led.

Although young and undisciplined, he would soon find
That the Army had need of his vigorous kind
Of encouraging others to fight, tooth and nail,
And not yield or retreat, not to falter or fail.

He didn't show fear but he understood that
Many others did not have the taste for combat
That he did – he knew discipline overcame fear
And could beat any enemy when it came near.

He knew fear was infectious, he'd seen the toughs run
On a wild Melbourne street at the sound of a gun
Or the sight of a phalanx of helmeted blue -
He knew fiery red could so quickly change hue.

To his folks he was Michael, to friends, simply Mick;
A lad, with his fists, so incredibly quick,
But as fast to pull back any punch when he saw
That his foe was defeated and, to him, might draw.

He had some about him who jumped when he spoke -
A loosely-held rabble the lad could invoke
To keep order of sorts in a criminal way -
The Police wouldn't act, but they weren't in his pay.

They just wouldn't accost him, they just let him be
For they knew he kept order, they'd no doubt that he
Would deal with any firebrands, using his chums -
McIntyre, the Menace of old Melbourne's slums.

But this menace in peacetime, in war, found a place
Fitted well to his nature and he would embrace
The demands of his training, the skills of his trade,
The need for precision when out on parade.

He was taught discipline and was very efficient
At directing assets and very proficient
Defeating the enemy when he appeared -
This killing machine was perfected and feared.

One stripe, he attracted, a second he earned
On the battlefield after superiors learned
Of his prowess with weapons, his way to exhort
All around him to fight without further support.

His third he would gain when his sergeant was killed
And he quickly took over in battle with skilled
And courageous deportment – the man wasn't meek -
He was made a Lieutenant the following week.

By custom, promotion to rank should have cost
Far more than he could raise, but his case wasn't lost
For someone had provided the money required -
A commission, with help from a friend, he acquired.

And that friend was Moran, an unspeakable rogue
Being kindred in spirit with battle in vogue.
He had funds to disperse and at oft time to waste
And, to grab those of others, was often in haste.

But that war wouldn't last long enough and would end
With an order that, homeward, the Army should send
All Colonial troops to where they had embarked
Just six short months before when hostilities sparked.

McIntyre was quite disappointed to go
But did not have the means to refuse and say *"No!"*
So Moran uttered to him, *"Keep in touch, My Good Chum.*
There'll be many more wars so do not sound so glum."

He'd return home from war as a leader of men,
Somewhat junior, no doubt, but somebody who, when
There had been call to duty, displayed not a flaw
Even though he was really escaping the Law.

But this was forgotten, interest had been lost
In the sins of his youth though they clearly had cost
More than one man his life – the Police had to cope
With more recent events – they'd forget him, he'd hope.

He'd become reinvented and rise above those
Who had once felt his fist when he chose to impose
His resolve, crude and vicious - the Police, as well -
But how far he could get was too early to tell.

Queen's Commission, he held, but no background to suit
The esteem due to rank – war had been the conduit
To a world he'd not known – he was barely equipped
To mix in with that class after, home, he was shipped.

But he had useful contacts to help him along
Though, to ask any more, he well knew would be wrong;
But his military record and rank would combine
With a natural talent he'd need to refine.

He would mingle with those of the Military set,
Be respectful and join in, but only when let;
He gained the employment such deference provides -
McIntyre, the thug, found that he had changed sides.

Not completely, of course; the man still had his ways
To finance his lifestyle, much like earlier days;
He would maintain his distance, his hands he kept clean
But, though playing the Gentleman, he was still mean.

In society, he would have felt out of place
For he was, to rise higher, just not in the race;
And although, in most places, the man could stand tall,
Melbourne, to McIntyre, felt very small.

But Moran came along, brought him into a fold
Set up for relieving the miners of Gold
In a gambling network which well could acquire
Any help from officialdom it might require.

This was just one of many, this great enterprise
Set up by Moriarty who must exercise
Great discretion while keeping the Gold flowing fast -
It was just one small part of an empire vast.

This Empire of Crime was stretched out the world wide.
It was firmly policed, rich enough to provide
All protection its people might need from the Law -
There was no way, however, for one to withdraw.

Contracted for life, each knew if he was tempted
And stole from the Master, he'd not be exempted
From giving that life, McIntyre was told -
He'd be very well paid to do just what he's told.

He'd have money to spend and a safe place to sleep -
As a friend of Moran, he was in very deep
With that Master of Crime he had promised to serve
And obey absolutely with every nerve.

He made special arrangements for each Army friend
Who might gamble and lose but find that, in the end,
He would win just enough to go home with a smile -
McIntyre was a natural for cunning and guile.

But then, on the death of his criminal master,
McIntyre perhaps saw a looming disaster.
He feared the protection which he had enjoyed
Would be gone and, quite soon, he might be unemployed.

But, as luck would have it, the African story
Once more needed telling by methods more gory
Than had been foreseen by a distant command -
The Boers were disgruntled and made their demand.

They were mobile, determined, and said that the soil
They stood on to be, by their efforts and toil,
A dominion, aside, by what they saw was right -
They declared independence and knew they must fight.

And, fight, the Boers would, although to no avail
As their efforts, courageous, were destined to fail
Due to sheer force of numbers and human attrition -
Such dreams, it would seem, would not come to fruition.

To declare independence, the timing was bad.
With Empire at its zenith, it was a poor lad
Who'd not run to the Colours to stand side-by-side
With his Empire brothers and, back-up, provide.

Colonial Australia had changed a great deal -
It had grown and matured, demanding a real
Stake at nationhood, proper – Federation, the call -
Each had called for contingents, six colonies, all.

They'd march out, these contingents, with rifle and pack,
Each one under the billowing Union Jack,
To declare that the Empire was theirs to defend -
On the rebels of Africa, they would descend.

But the Boers were not rebels, in their eyes, at least,
And they thought of the Empire as some rampant beast
Come to force, on their countrymen, rules of a sort
Which would render the Treaty a scandalous rort.

Fighting over home ground, the Boers took a high toll,
First upon Spion Kop, a notorious knoll
Which would be a bad portent of actions to come -
Misery for the soldier but glory for some.

McIntyre then returned to the colours of old
Though he did have his eyes set on African Gold;
He'd received no instructions at all from Moran -
He did not even know how to contact the man.

The war proved quite a boon for this soldier who thrived
In the turmoil of battle for, since he arrived
On a transport ship heavy with soldiers and mounts,
McIntyre remembered that victory counts.

In his first week, Boer skirmishers challenged the line
Deep inside friendly territory up an incline
Thought, by many, too steep and too rough to traverse -
Surprised, sleepy guards all began to disperse.

This, of course, was the way to concede a defeat.
McIntyre, however, called out to entreat
All his comrades to arms, to stand firm and to fight
And to put the Boers down or to put them to flight.

He grabbed up his carbine and bandolier, full,
Thrust his feet in his boots and then charged like a bull
At the Boers causing havoc and stemmed their advance
Giving, to all assailed, a fair fighting chance.

Fragments of a bullet, though, pieced the man's chest
But he fought on regardless, not stopping to rest
And, though all superficial, his wounds were infected -
Until they'd turned septic, they went undetected.

He went down with a fever, confined to a bed,
On his back for a while but the Boers had all fled;
The fever would have him laid out for its term -
He had fought back the Boers but went down to a germ.

He was sick for a week with a temperature, high;
He would rally, though death seemed apparently nigh.
He'd demand the return of his horse and his gun -
He would not want to miss one more day of the fun.

He was not quite the fellow he'd been in his youth -
A great deal more polished and not so uncouth
But, also, not as robust and physically strong -
To attempt to recover that man would be wrong.

But the man was outrageously vain in his manner
And sought out adventure – he held high his banner
As much to be seen both by foe and by friend
As it was for the ego he sought to defend.

But, at last, he recovered enough to arise
From his hospital bed and to duly advise
All the doctors that he was as fit as required
And to be with his comrades was what he desired.

He'd been made Brevet Major, a senior rank
But a temporary one and for which he could thank
His own presence and daring when wounded in battle -
He had men fight like tigers, not run off like cattle.

That the war would be bitter, he knew to be true
But, whatever his motives, he was of the hue
To regather his strength, requisition a mount,
And go off to the front where his presence would count.

There were battles and skirmishes, bloody and grand,
But the war-gods were fickle and chose to demand
That the Boers be defeated, despite their resolve,
And Transvaal would, around Britain's axis, revolve.

In the background of turmoil, stood Colonel Moran,
Late of Dartmoor, the prison, renewing the span
Of another empire, a kingdom of crime -
Two times he'd been beaten – he'd triumph this time.

He had failed at Reichenbach, then killed Adair
But was foiled by Sherlock and breathed the cold air
Of the dismal Old Dart, but escaped with a plan
Which required the daring of one special man.

Well, that man, McIntyre, was keen for a fight.
With end of the war with the Boers now in sight
He was keen to proceed, in some manner, toward
Any action to give him substantial reward.

Many units were now being repatriated -
McIntyre's also, even though he fixated
On fighting an enemy beaten and starved,
Their lands, into parcels of real estate, carved.

McIntyre's exploits, African, yielded much -
It was not, perhaps, glory, but infamy such
That his name, through the territory, became known -
His name, with its harsh reputation, had grown.

McIntyre, again, would miss out on the spoils
And a man such as he would be one who recoils
At the thought that his efforts might just be bought off
With a few shiny medals – at that he would scoff.

His ego felt cheated; he also resumed
His old rank of Lieutenant – he'd hoped and presumed
He'd be given a posting reflecting his actions
But lost out to the Empire's upper-crust factions.

Months before, he had gotten a letter quite strange
From an old Army comrade who said he'd arrange,
In due course, were he interested, something to suit
His particular talents, something to bear fruit.

It was sent by Moran whom he thought executed,
Although learning the sentence of death was commuted
To life behind bars – obviously he'd escaped
And was free, in a whole new identity, draped.

Moran's agents moved in and appraised him of facts
Of a plan which would have catastrophic impacts
On the world as a whole - there were battles to fight
Which just might give a fellow like him great delight.

Sweet vengeance, although not a promise was broken,
McIntyre could have on the British whose token
Reward was a medal – he felt he'd earned more
And he eagerly sought what Moran had in store.

THE VOYAGE

McIntyre was told to take leave of his men,
Proceed rapidly to Port Elizabeth, then
He should seek out a letter addressed 'M. McBride'
At the Post Office, local – instructions inside.

This would go against orders he had from the Crown;
He would also be letting his countrymen down
Making him a pariah in exile with no
Way back into their favour – home, he couldn't go.

He would have to sneak out under cover of dark
And, upon active service, this would leave a mark
Which could not be removed by his record or fame -
McIntyre was playing a dangerous game.

"You should forego your uniform, make no allusion
To military matters – there'll be much confusion
With types coming in with the war nearly finished
Set to pick clean a carcase with danger diminished."

"There, a boat which awaits your arrival, you'll seek.
It will not be a steamer but, rather, a sleek
Yankee schooner to take you to where you'll change ship
At a place you'll discover half-way through your trip."

"Its name and location you'll learn from the letter.
It isn't in code but the Boss thought it better
To have this concealed in a jumble of chatter -
You know who that is so you'll know what will matter."

"The letter you get, open up at the Port.
The Colonel says that you are not of the sort
Who would go against orders – do not let him down -
He's not very forgiving, so don't make him frown."

"On the schooner, more letters – don't open them yet.
The one marked 'M1' open up when you get
To your first fall of land – it tells you of your quest -
But 'M2' leave for now – just enjoy a good rest."

"That one marked 'M2' you must give to a man
Known to us – you must find him as soon as you can
When you get where you're going as detailed inside
That letter 'M1' the Captain will provide."

McIntyre then acceded – he'd do as requested.
A voyage at sea might see him fully rested -
The effects of his infected wounds lingered, still,
Causing fevers which tore at his strength and his will.

Port Elizabeth took two full days to be reached -
It was full of old steamers and barges all beached
Well away from where transports were all being loaded
With troops going home - none needed being goaded.

Fresh arrivals were milling around in confusion
While Sergeants were shouting to all a profusion
Of orders, while Corporals pushed men into lines.
Strutting officers were bristling like porcupines.

McIntyre detrained and proceeded to find
The Post Office while he, always, had to remind
Himself that he was sought like the Boers he pursued,
Though he was, with the stain of deserter, imbued.

He had papers provided to name him McBride -
Documents of identity which would provide
Him with what he would need to collect Moran's mail -
For the rest he'd need nerve if he was to prevail.

With the Post Office found and his letter collected,
McIntyre discovered Moran had selected
A schooner named Swordfish whose Captain and crew,
Every tract of the southernmost waters, well knew.

He would find it was anchored far out in the bay
And was told that a seaman called Marcus O'Shay
Would be found at Two-thirty on each afternoon
Over three days precisely – he must find him soon.

O'Shay would wait under the Post Office tower -
He could be recognised as a man of great power
And size and would carry a large coil of rope –
He should ask him the way to the Cape of Good Hope.

McIntyre found O'Shay on the very first day
And the pair was soon hurrying down to the bay
To hop into a dinghy then row to the schooner -
For McIntyre, leaving just couldn't come sooner.

When on board he was greeted and shown to his bunk
By the Captain who'd shifted a great pile of junk
From the tiniest cabin he ever had seen -
It was dry and was private if he drew a screen.

The Captain then gave him two envelopes, sealed;
What 'M1' contained could be only revealed
When he opened the seal at his first destination -
He was told, "*It's Hawaii.*" without hesitation.

"*It's American territory, now, you might know,*
For the U.S. decided to take it in tow
In the year '98." so the Captain explained,
"*So there would be no reason to have you detained.*"

'M2', the next envelope, was for a man
To be identified after he'd had time to scan
The contents of the first – he must bide well his time,
Make the best of his lodgings, his mind he must prime.

Sails set, the Swordfish then proceeded at speed
To the east, to head under Australia, though need
Might dictate that it stop at some point for more stores
On the furthest extent of those southernmost shores.

They were off to Hawaii and boldly displaying
The Stars and the Stripes of America praying
The winds would be with them – delay would be bad
For the Captain and crew and their eager nomad.

They'd cross over the sea-lanes which led to the place
He called home but which now held the man in disgrace.
All his bridges were burnt, he was now cast adrift
Though Moran said he'd give him Melbourne as a gift.

McIntyre knew Moran and his gift of the gab
But he thought it worthwhile that he might have a stab
At the fabulous treasures that might well be gained -
Such delusions of grandeur the man entertained.

But the weather was set for clear sailing and, so,
It was straight to Hawaii the Swordfish would go
And deposit its passenger on its arrival -
McIntyre would often despair of survival.

Compared to the transports, the schooner was light
And its Captain, it seemed, took the greatest delight
In attacking the waves as it cut through the surge
Of the great Southern Ocean with unfailing urge.

The Forties were rough to a landlubber sort
Such as McIntyre was – he would long for a port
Where the waters were placid, the waves all restrained -
But it did him no good if he ever complained.

Up and down went the Swordfish, oft-times on a list
And his stomach went with it – he had to resist
The temptation to jump overboard and swim back
As the schooner relentlessly flew at full tack.

At last they had travelled Australia's length -
McIntyre thought he might recover his strength.
The Captain announced they'd be veering north-east
McIntyre, however, could care not the least.

They were into the Tasman but waters remained
Fairly rough but the winds were a little restrained
And the progress was slower but, still, the ship bounced
Up and down like a cork being battered and trounced.

Their route took them far past the northerly tip
Of New Zealand's north island just trying to clip
A few hours, perhaps days, from his previous best
Time of passage – the crew would have no time to rest.

There'd be atolls to dodge for a while till the swell
Of the wide open ocean, to all, formed to tell
Of the start of straight sailing till they saw the cloud
High above Mount Ka'ela, a banner held proud.

They would slow as the heaviest sheets would be struck
From their masts as the sailors considered their luck
For another safe passage, then waited as tide
Would permit, into harbour, a slow steady ride.

Honolulu was named for its waters being calm
And could promise the shade of a sheltering palm
From a hot blazing sun when a man stepped ashore -
McIntyre, that Swordfish, had grown to deplore.

Back on land he would curse every sailor he saw
But, of course, to himself - it would be the last straw
To be drawn to a fight when his strength was so low
That he'd hardly be able to strike one a blow.

So, he'd keep a low profile and open the sealed
Envelope marked 'M1' to find what it revealed
About what next to do, about where he should go -
If it mentioned a schooner, he'd like to say "*No.*".

He sat on a bench and looked far out to sea
At the ships in the distance and made a short plea
That whatever 'M1' would be found to contain,
It would, from any mention of sailing, refrain.

'M1' mentioned a vessel, it said the Sea Quest
Steamed regularly out from America's west
To Hawaii with tourists and general cargo
Ten times every year out of San Francisco.

The Swordfish's voyage was timed so it should
Coincide with the Sea Quest's and therefore he would
After just a few days be on board and away
To the Golden Gate into San Francisco bay.

There he'd seek out a man who was known to Moran
And would give him 'M2' which detailed a plan
Which had once been prepared by the Master of Crime
And was now resurrected – he mustn't waste time.

Murphy was his name, his address was detailed -
A glad McIntyre read "steamed" and not "sailed".
He would seek out the ship and book passage and wait -
It felt like he was fishing but he was the bait.

But he was used to orders which didn't make sense
At the time they were given – but still he was tense
For he felt the effects of his voyage and feared
That his long bouts of fever had not disappeared.

He inquired and found that the Sea Quest was due
To depart in two days – he had time to subdue
The imbalance he felt and the horrible notion
Hawaii was floating and in constant motion.

Perhaps if he walked and explored the whole town
He might just keep the worst of his imbalance down.
He would walk up and down Honolulu's main street
Till Hawaii no longer rolled under his feet.

The two days went by slowly, his walks helped a bit
And, to walk up the gangway, he felt he was fit.
His cabin, he found, was a major improvement -
He had room to stretch and he felt little movement.

With its boilers afire and its steam pressure high,
McIntyre could swear that he heard the ship sigh
As its single propeller rotated and thrust
The ship out to the ocean - a calm one, he'd trust.

McIntyre, while en-route, felt his temperature rise
And knew what to expect – it would be no surprise
To this veteran of Africa's life-sapping heat
That a fever was coming, though one he would beat.

There would be a few days of discomfort and pain
In his joints and his head, and he knew that his brain
Would run through all his battles, his moments of strife,
Bringing all of his subconscious demons to life.

He had tinctures to take for the pain which he knew
Would make him quite sleepy – he'd ask one of the crew
To bring him lots of water and never pay heed
To whatever he'd say about any foul deed.

Worst of all, close to home port, a definite chop
On the waters developed – he hoped it would stop
But the waves just got bigger – they'd entered a storm.
McIntyre found this, out at sea, was the norm.

He was sea-sick again but his fever subsided
A little and he would at times be provided
With water and tincture – at last the sea stilled -
McIntyre, for one, was decidedly thrilled.

He was still in the last throws of fever when he
Heard the call from a sailor to rise and come see
For the Golden Gate passage had come into view -
San Francisco was home port for much of the crew.

The ship had to wait for the fog to disperse.
McIntyre found some little time to converse
With the sailors on board and hear what they would say
Of the town they called home they had come to today.

The ship made its way slowly while sounding its horn,
Penetrating and long, sounding very forlorn
As the lookouts kept watch and the Captain held steady,
His engine room crew, to reverse, ever ready.

Now inside the Bay and with fog thinning out
And beginning to lift, one man gave out a shout:
"There she is, it's Old Frisco.", then ran to the rail
To see steamships, all new, amid veterans of sail.

As the fog banks retreated, the funnels and masts,
Row by row, appeared slowly - the long probing blasts
From steam whistles and foghorns all faded away
As the ship powered into St Francis' Bay.

Past the Alcatraz lighthouse, the prison and fort,
On that Island of Pelicans, now last resort
Of the felon most evil, unruly, depraved -
McIntyre looked on and defiantly waved.

On The Rock, the new prison was said to be grim,
Proof against all escape even if one could swim
Because strong flowing currents and sharks on patrol
Kept the prisoners land-bound and under control.

He thought to himself that a man would be wise
To steer clear of all trouble and so exercise
Great discretion in Frisco – no demons unlock -
He could not, unlike pelicans, fly from The Rock.

He then felt a spasm of pain in his head
And he felt that he'd rather be sleeping instead
Of preparing to visit the contact Moran
Had described as his West Coast America man.

The bouts of the fever were now lasting longer
And coming more quickly and seemingly stronger
Than they had before – he remembered the cold
Words of warning once given: *"You're getting too old."*

"Too old for the life which you've chosen to follow."
A doctor had told him. Those words sounded hollow
To one who had made grown men quiver in dread.
"Keep on as you've been and you soon will be dead."

Laudanum was his crutch and at times he would lean
On it ever so heavily making him mean
And, at times, unpredictably prone to assail
Anyone who annoyed him – control could be frail.

But he felt strength returning and when the ship docked,
To his contact, he'd hurry, his mind now unblocked
From effects of the Laudanum, or so he thought -
He perhaps was proceeding faster than he ought.

THE PROPOSITION

Down the gangway he'd stride with his papers to show
To officials who'd check them although he would know
That they had been approached and persuaded to let
Him pass freely through Customs with little upset.

He would then proceed swiftly to where he'd contact
His American colleague and try to extract
An agreement to join in a great enterprise
Which only that Master of Crime could devise.

He climbed onto a cab which would transport him where
He might meet with his contact, that's if he was there
At the time he arrived – he'd at least leave his card -
He hoped finding the fellow would not be too hard.

It was easy, in fact, for luck stuck to his side
And the address he gave was a ten minute ride
From the docks where he'd landed. Murphy was within.
McIntyre, however, then felt his head spin.

He did not need a spasm when meeting the man
Who had been recommended by Colonel Moran.
His lightness of head he'd fight off, so he thought,
And walked in to meet Murphy, the man he had sought.

49

Murphy stood, and he offered a greeting, polite,
"Sit down, if you please, I have no appetite
For excessive formality – your card I've received
And you've business to offer, if I'm not deceived."

"I was told to expect you – I do know your name
And, before you, has travelled your African fame.
But you seem somewhat queasy, so please take a seat.
I'm afraid it's quite humid, our Frisco Bay heat."

Then Murphy continued as Mack took his chair,
"You haven't had time to get used to our air."
He then asked a question which left Mack quite shaken -
"Your accent – it's English, unless I'm mistaken."

"It's English, it's not," Mack declared with offence
In his manner and voice, *"and I'll ask that you, hence,*
Speak of me as Australian – of that, I insist -
You'll learn what that means if, with slights, you persist."

McIntyre jumped up, pushed his chair far aside -
A fair bit of fighting room this would provide.
Murphy, flabbergasted, alarmed, took a stance
Quite defensive and shouted, while he had the chance:

"Well, don't jump down my throat like a mad kangaroo -
I just can't tell the difference - the accents are too
Close together for my ears to say which is which
And to threaten somebody for that's a bit rich."

"Well, I'm Irish," declared McIntyre, composed,
"I'm not a mad Fenian but I'm supposed
To stand up for myself in a quite manly way
So do not call me English, especially today."

"Me, likewise," said Murphy, *"but it doesn't follow
I'd recognise accents - that argument's hollow.
I suggest we sit down and discuss what we must -
We'll have no more misunderstandings, I trust."*

*"I'm as Irish as you but, like you, I have never
Set foot on the Emerald Isle, not ever.
We have much to talk over and much to prepare -
If you're English or Irish or not, I don't care."*

McIntyre knew that he had made a mistake -
A quite serious one, but he must stay awake
And retain his composure – this man was no fool -
He must get his temper to settle and cool.

*"I'm from Melbourne in fact, but in Africa served
And my travels have left me a little unnerved,
Especially the last several days on a boat
In a storm when I feared it would not stay afloat."*

*"I had suffered from fever before I embarked
And the storm we encountered apparently sparked
An internal reaction I couldn't control -
It's something I caught on the Veldt on patrol."*

*"I most earnestly beg your indulgence for my
Unforgivable outburst – I rarely would fly
Off the handle like that but, with nerves at full stretch,
For no reason I reacted just like a wretch."*

Murphy retook his seat and then indicated
To McIntyre, now somewhat humiliated,
That he should sit, too, which he did rather shyly;
Murphy then spoke up in a manner quite wryly:

"We'll say no more about it, so, when you're composed
I will pour you a drink, that is, if you're disposed
To strong liquor, of course – our whistles need wetting
And you would not object to a whiskey, I'm betting."

McIntyre then watched as two glasses were filled
To the brim over which just a little was spilled.
"You're too generous, Friend, after how I behaved -
After how I jumped up like a demon depraved."

Murphy handed a glass to his curious guest
Saying, *"No more of that. So, now, here's to the best*
For us both in whatever the future may find.
Now tell me, My Friend, what do you have in mind?"

McIntyre, composed, took a sip from his glass,
Having said *"Best of health!"*, as his temper had passed
From outrageously stupid to fiendishly cool -
He would keep his composure and not act the fool.

"Well, your name had been given to me by a friend
Who's dealt with you before and who would recommend
Any work you have done, any services rendered,
As well worth any payment, to you, that he'd tendered."

"I give value for money though, cheap, I am not.
I'm not carried away by some fabulous plot
Far too good to be true." Murphy stated distinctly.
"I'm nobody's fool." he then stated succinctly.

"How might you describe him – that friend? Could it be
That his name starts with 'M', if he is known to me?"
Murphy asked keeping all expectations contained
While he tested his guest in a manner constrained.

"Well, it's 'M' that it is, and a Colonel he's been
Wearing bright British red sitting squarely between
His desire and duty – Moran is his name."
McIntyre declared, well aware of his fame.

"A good man in a tussle." said Murphy, agreeing,
"But he is in prison unless they've been freeing
Those convicts who somehow evaded the noose.
Are you here to tell me that Moran's on the loose?"

"Well, as far as the prison authorities know,
He is safe in a cell which is way down below
In a place most secure till his dying day."
McIntyre replied, *"But perhaps he's away."*

"Away with the Devil, perhaps, but he's out
Of his cell, none-the-less, and he's now right about
Doing all he can do to bring plans into play
Which will bring, to our rivals, a reckoning day."

"The first stage is completed – that part of the plan
Was to draw, to the Moors and destruction, the man
Who alone could have stopped us – nobody else would
For nobody was able to see what he could."

"Well, that is reassuring. His presence alone
Could, around Moran's neck, hang a heavy millstone
Or perhaps place a noose." Murphy said in reply,
"You link with Moran - I would like to know why."

"He's ex-Indian Army, if I'm not mistaken.
How is it your African path's overtaken
A man whose career had been Subcontinental?
Were your dealings commercial or just regimental?"

"Well, a little of both, but much more of the first.
Though we did meet in uniform, he had a thirst
For adventure mixed in with some extra incentive."
McIntyre replied, *"The man's quite inventive."*

"That would be twenty years ago, or thereabouts,
When we both were attached to an odd group of scouts
Who could search and report or attack and destroy
Using whatever tactics it chose to employ."

"Understand this was not against Boers, as today;
We were fighting the Zulus and needed to stay
Well away from their numbers – those fellows could run
And would soon be upon us – that wouldn't be fun."

"But, in due course, some practical bargains were struck
With the chieftains and, as it would be our luck,
Our group was disbanded and I was sent packing
Though, for me, I can't say that fortune was lacking."

"I was raised up from Private to officer rank
And our Colonel Moran is the one I must thank
For that rise, unbelievable – truly I must -
The one thing we do have is mutual trust."

"We'd met up again since that time we had parted.
In Melbourne by mail, then twice since we started
Our recent adventures – again, a great fight,
But this time against Boers, but we put them to flight."

"You fought them to a standstill - those men didn't run.
They submitted with families under the gun."
Replied Murphy, who'd kept up with overseas news
Feigning great sympathy when expressing his views.

"That is true." McIntyre agreed, *"But you'd know*
War is dirty no matter how generals might crow
About honour and duty and courage and grit -
I thought you'd be the type who would not care a bit."

"We're adventurers, all, as a type, you and me.
And Moran is as well, and another who'd be
At the head of our enterprise, if he weren't dead,
So Moran is the man who will lead in his stead."

"And that man who is dead – can you give me a name?"
Murphy cagily asked recognising the game
McIntyre was playing and doing his best -
The question he asked was by way of a test.

McIntyre gave Murphy an all-knowing look
And he grinned as his head, in a knowing way, shook,
"He is dead but is still never mentioned by those
Who, for tightness of lip, he deliberately chose."

"We all share an initial, that's all I can say,
And that's all that I will. So, I've come here today
With a firm proposition from him who's in charge -
The prospects are Golden, rewards very large."

"I've a document here in my pocket in code
And I'm told to tell you it's in Astrakhan mode
Which means nothing to me but to you will be clear -
The man who has sent me could well be quite near."

"I'm to leave it here with you – you must make a sign
As detailed in the message if you would align
Yourself with him, in full, in what he proposes -
Of course, there is more than the message discloses."

"If your answer is 'Yes' we must travel quite soon.
Your advice in such matters would be a great boon
For America, to me, presents a blank sheet
But a native like you must know every street."

"Well, perhaps I exaggerate, but hear me out.
Moran is a man whose words we can't flout.
He just lives to give orders – so, if you'd say 'No'
Say it first, say it once, or your life you'll forego."

"I do know the ways of your Colonel Moran -
They are not quite the same as that other great man
Who had plunged to his death in a great waterfall.
But I, too, can take orders and give them my all."

Murphy grinned just a little and stretched out his hand
Saying to McIntyre, by way of demand,
"Just give the thing to me then I will decide,
When I've read it, if I want to play on his side."

McIntyre reached into his coat pocket and
Withdrew 'M2' while making a overly grand
Gesture handing it over – Murphy then broke the seal,
And would study the message within with a great zeal.

He read through the coded proposal with speed
And he said, *"I have interest in this scheme, indeed.*
With Moran on the loose and the network renewed,
There'll be potions delicious about to be brewed."

"I can travel to Britain – four weeks, it will take.
That is so unbelievable I have to shake
My head knowing that once it would take half a year.
But we'll need to leave soon – that's abundantly clear."

"First, to New York by train then to London by ship.
If fortune's on our side and we don't make a slip
We can do it. I need a few days to prepare -
We'll travel together; I'll cover your fare."

"I had thought Moran gone to a place where he'd not
Have a chance to regather his forces and plot
Out a scheme on a scale worth any great risk.
His message in code tells me I must be brisk."

"I had once been a factor he chose to employ
And we once met in person – his trust I enjoy.
We agreed on a code which we called Astrakhan
So I do know that message had come from Moran."

"But, his nemesis – what of that Great Interferer,
Or should I just call him the Great Perseverer.
We once thought him dead but he turned up alive -
If there's one thing he can do, the man can survive."

"Ah, yes. Sherlock Holmes. The name sticks in my craw
And his interference would have been the last straw.
He has suffered of late, people laugh at his name,"
McIntyre declared, *"and he's out of the game."*

Murphy looked at his guest with a quizzical stare
While he thought, to himself, if he really might dare
To believe it were so and the stage would be cleared
Of that odious hero when villains appeared.

"I would like to think so, but I've heard that before.
The man hasn't appeared on our Pacific Shore
But we read of his exploits out here in the West -
If someone needs an enemy, he is the best."

"Well, the best is now bested, he's down on his knees
And is way out of London and playing with bees."
McIntyre said, laughing, *"Moran saw to that.*
On his face, the Great Meddler fell heavy and flat."

THE RISK

It was true Holmes had faltered and fell on one knee
But his mind, in due course, would be able to free
Itself of all confusion, of thoughts highly jumbled -
He had not fallen flat on his face, only stumbled.

Several menacing M's were against him, though one
Was there only in spirit – he had come undone
At the Reichenbach Falls but had laid out a scheme
Which even he thought to be far too extreme.

But Moran knew its detail, potential and scope
Though was not wise enough to accept that the hope
Of its gifted creator to own all he saw
Was, in fact, in itself, a most serious flaw.

Moriarty knew well that to succeed he must
Not attract much attention but seem to be just
A Professor pursuing the nature of things
While he sat, safe and sound, pulling criminal strings.

If that plan was to come to fruition, he would
Attract much more attention than anyone should
Who'd remain undiscovered while ruling in stealth
And amassing, in secret, great power and wealth.

Such an audacious plan had no chance to succeed
If its perpetrators would been blinded by greed
Or the need to be noticed – to be vain was to fail
And the effort it took would to be no avail.

But the worst flaw of all was a mind highly keen
Which was able to see just how evil had been
And how widespread the Empire of Crime had become.
Such a mind could disrupt a successful outcome.

Sherlock Holmes had that mind which was able to see
Such an Empire existed while functioning free
Of suspicion of being any threat to the nation -
The Great Sleuth represented a great complication.

And that great complication might best be removed
If that man, Sherlock Holmes, could be soundly reproved
By a scheme which would get him to venture away
From his regular haunts and to be led astray.

To have killed Sherlock Holmes was to validate all
He had said about organised crime – they would fall
From the pressure that public opinion would bring
To denounce and to topple the criminal king.

Moriarty had never considered the plan
To be workable although he said to Moran
That if ever he did put the plan into action
He'd provide Sherlock Holmes with a major distraction.

"That distraction," he said, *"had to draw him away*
From the Metropolis to somewhere we can play
With his mind and to somehow discredit him fully -
We must make the man look a fool and a bully."

Moran took this on-board and would long for the time
When his Master would unleash the ultimate crime.
When his Master was killed and his network destroyed,
Moran, with its implementation, had toyed.

Moran thought he'd take over – he knew everyone
And he knew everything Moriarty had done.
What was left of the networks he'd try to repair
But was caught as a card cheat by Ronald Adair.

The events which ensued saw Moran put away
For his natural life although, without delay,
He began pulling strings of his own from his cell -
How long it would hold him, nobody could tell.

By a bribe or a threat he would sneak past the bars
And began to contact those dispersed petty czars
But was careful to always appear locked away
While some networks of old were brought back into play.

Sherlock was, for a while, hopeful of a reprieve
From such networks – he did have the right to believe
That, with Moran locked up, his old Master dead,
The streets around London were safer to tread.

It was springtime, of sorts, as the felons he knew
Were more readily tracked and the escapees few;
There had been more convictions with no one to swear
Alibis for the guilty – their fates they must wear.

There was Watson, as well, a large factor to count
In the workings of Sherlock - the man could amount
To a force on his own, counting felons detained,
Though he had, from accepting the credit, refrained.

He did not have the instincts which Sherlock possessed
And was not a free agent, he often confessed,
But owed duty to patients, also to his wife -
His was leading, in truth, a quite composite life.

But the man had raw courage and often had stood
Side by side with his colleague, both agents of Good
Against Evil, and caused their opponents to yield -
He would not use his friend, Sherlock Holmes, as a shield.

For, together, their worth was increased many-fold.
They had stared down, in unison, many a cold
Blooded killer and brought him to face consequences -
A short hempen rope or a place with high fences.

In the field, Watson's worth was expressed in his sound
Grasp of medical knowledge, for often they'd found
A poor victim near death who would then be revived
By the skills brought to bear when John Watson arrived.

Sherlock's mind operated with fractions of facts -
From a little hint here; over there old impacts
Of the hooves of a horse overloaded; a twig
Freshly broken – all might point to something quite big.

John Watson, however, to give him his due
Was, at times, just as able to pick up a clue
But would rarely be able to see any link -
He needed full facts when the time came to think.

This could be used against this most dangerous pair
For, if one could get Sherlock away from the air
And the jumble of London, his natural ground,
A chink in their armour could likely be found.

And that chink might be found in the different ways
Each one thought – for the logical mind always sways
Back and forth with a problem until it is solved
While for minds such as Watson's, that's far too involved.

If they fed him with facts set against common sense,
Sherlock Holmes might be made to become very tense
At his own loss of logic – to rebel, his mind might,
Leading him, with his colleague, to argue and fight.

Moran pondered this and he knew Holmes had not
Ever viewed Moriarty in death, so a plot
Might succeed if he got Holmes insisting, instead,
Moriarty somehow had come back from the dead.

If that's all which Holmes' logical mind would accept,
He would state it as definite, sounding inept
To his friends and his colleagues, Police and the Press -
Sherlock Holmes would be put under mounting duress.

This, of course, came to be and Holmes had to retire
For old friends kept their distance - he had to acquire
A brand-new set of skills which allowed his great mind
To mull over clues of a much different kind.

He, for months, honed apiarian skills he'd declared
Would be used in retirement when he prepared
To desist in detection, consulting to cease,
His old life, however, took on a new lease.

He went back to London, his spirit renewed
And reborn, fully ready to see what had brewed
On the streets of old London since he'd been away -
He was back in his element and back to stay.

But, of course, few had known of that spirit reborn
In the Greatest Detective who seemed to have torn,
From his mind, all the demons which troubled it so -
He was right back in business and ready to go.

He had seen that a note had been tacked to his door
Placing doubt in his mind of that menacing moor
And the agent of darkness behind the events
Meant to push his Great Mind to its utter extents.

But that mind was resilient and would rebound
And it would, to all doubters, prove well to be sound.
And when back in his element, like days of old,
Holmes discovered the whole thing was all about Gold.

Upon seeing the note and its taunting content
Sherlock felt that it could be a new challenge sent
By whoever had caused the moor's outrages, grim,
Hoping that it would get between Watson and him.

He and Watson decided that they'd play along
With the taunt while, in secret, they'd send out a strong
Call for help from their allies – all Sherlock would say
Was *"The game is afoot and I'm ready to play."*

"Underestimate Holmes at your peril." he'd state
As he pondered the puzzle and his recent fate.
Every felon would know that his words were sincere -
Holmes was eager to meddle and would interfere.

This was what Moriarty had feared for his plan
For he knew very well that if any one man
Could upset all his planning, Holmes would be his name
So he had to be taken right out of the game.

Moran knew very well of this great limitation.
Sherlock Holmes was, of course, Moriarty's fixation
As the only one able to think as he did
So he would, like his Master, of Sherlock, be rid.

But Sherlock just wouldn't succumb to the ruse
On the Moors for too long – he returned home to use
His spectacular powers of reasoned deduction
While Moran and his plan suffered utter destruction.

With the aid of his colleague and friends, Sherlock sought
Out the meaning of many factors which he thought
Might be leading to something disastrously large -
Sherlock Holmes, into danger, was ready to charge.

But, of course, Sherlock's history was one of success
Even though he would go to great pains to confess
That he had, at times, failed when seeking a clue
Which evaded his eyes – then derision was due.

He was very pragmatic, success was his aim;
Humility wasn't a virtue he'd claim
For he valued the truth and would run it to ground
In a manner he knew that was sure to astound.

If his method was clever, he'd say it was so;
To be self-deprecating, he'd always say "*No*"
Unless he had felt that a failure was his
And he might well have said: "*Tell it just how it is.*"

Moran played for high stakes and it brought him undone
In the past when he fell to the efforts of one
Who had him sent to prison to linger and stew -
Moran had learned some lessons, but did miss a few.

Moran was a gambler and hunter and saw
Every crime as a thrilling exploit and a raw
Game of sport to be tackled with planning and nerve -
But the man didn't have Moriarty's reserve.

With a plan so audacious, one needed restraint
Till the plan was in action – Moran would acquaint
His subordinates with many vital details
Which were better kept secret, else everything fails.

But Moran brought two fellows to help implement
The grand plan, but he wasn't able to prevent
One demanding the facts which he felt he deserved.
McIntyre's insistence left Murphy unnerved.

Murphy was quite stable – he knew how to hold
His tongue firmly when discussing matters of Gold.
He took orders as given and gave them in turn -
McIntyre, such obedience, would often spurn.

Murphy was allotted his part of the plan
Which would be implemented whenever Moran
Gave the order to move – he did not need to know
More detail than that – discipline, he must show.

McIntyre insisted in knowing much more -
As a soldier he felt that he should know the score
When it came to him facing a danger unknown -
He'd insist that, the entire plan, he'd be shown.

Moran trusted the man with his life but he knew
McIntyre's response, were he able to view
The whole plan – he might want to be in on the action
At every stage to his own satisfaction.

Discipline might be lost and the scheme come to nought
But Mack did have the guts and the nerve that he sought.
He would give McIntyre an overview, brisk,
But, in doing so, he took a terrible risk.

THE GLITTER

The root of all evil, so goes the old saying,
Is blind love of money, so often betraying
A weakness of character, heartless and cold,
Made worse when encountering glittering Gold.

That glitter of Gold and the promise it gave
Anyone who was able and ready to brave
All the danger presented and obstacles struck
Would make many dump reason and resort to luck.

Gold deposits were scarce and were most often found
By some lucky explorers surveying the ground
Of an opening frontier few others had seen
And on which even fewer would ever have been.

The frontier had presented a challenge to those
Who, to step into danger, all willingly chose
Knowing well most would fail and some not return -
Struck down by Gold Fever, such cares they would spurn.

There'd been rushes before to grab Gold from the land
But, of late, there had been overwhelming demand
And the means to move people as never before
And some regions were shaken right down to the core.

Many towns were depleted of men, strong and fit,
As, in droves, they were smitten and just up and quit.
Factory owners would flounder and farmers would fail -
They all called their men fools but to no great avail.

California was truly the first great Gold rush
And saw thousands leave home and relentlessly crush
Onto any train leaving and heading out west -
These men were the strongest and often the best.

Some men gave up early while some struck it rich -
There was little to foretell which man would be which
For it often came down to willpower and pluck
And, in so many cases, a good bit of luck.

And those with that luck got the best to be found -
Easy pickings from diggings, or just off the ground.
Others looked to the streams for alluvial dust
Panned from gravels and sands with a devilish lust.

Elbow to elbow, the men lined the streams
Or dug deeper and deeper fulfilling their dreams.
But the Gold to be gotten by pick or by pan
Would be quickly depleted by those in the van.

Some who followed behind found fair pickings as well
But as numbers exploded the odds quickly fell
That the typical miner, though able and plucky,
Might stake out a claim and would then strike it lucky.

With their Gold, some retired and lived a life, high;
Some just wasted their fortunes and then, with a sigh,
Went on back to the diggings to reclaim the dream
Of that soft Yellow Metal, its glitter and gleam.

Like ants on an anthill put under some threat,
Miners scurried around, digging holes by the sweat
Of their backs and their brows till the Gold was all gone
And, with it, the sunshine which, on their dreams shone.

But across the Pacific was heard a great shout -
There was Gold in Australia and nuggets would sprout
From the ground to be grabbed by the first on the scene
With nobody who would or who could intervene.

First the east then the south then the west yielded more
Of that most precious metal as many men swore
They would come home a prince, not a pauper in rags -
There was Gold to be had to be brought home in bags.

Further westward, more land showed the metallic glint
Of that maker of dreams and, then, as the first hint
Of its presence leaked out and the fever took hold,
The world started digging for Africa's Gold.

But officialdom struck bringing in regulation -
Big business took over and then speculation
Became the device to pour ever more money
To seek out that metal the colour of honey.

Governments issued licences, all for a price
Far too high, most had thought, representing a slice
Very thick of the cake earned by toil and sweat -
Men in uniform moved in and issued a threat.

The small miner was pushed to the limits and found
He was wasting his time digging up barren land
So he took to the road and the rail and departed
For places his dream could, again, be restarted.

Such events were repeated, results were the same.
It was like life was playing some devilish game
With the miners who took all the risk but were robbed -
But upon hearing "*Gold!*", every steamer was mobbed.

Yet again, men would hear it, that siren-like call
From a distance compelling the smitten to fall
Into line and go forth and make war on the land -
Those hearing the call would submit to demand.

The Gold-bearing regions were temperate or torrid,
Sometimes hot, sometimes chilly but never so horrid
That men weren't enticed to down tools and go forth,
But then came the call from the cold frozen north.

From the wilds of Alaska, the whisper of Gold
Drew more men to the region in spite of the cold
And the danger to life in those northerly lands
Which would, on any weakness, make fatal demands.

Mining madness took over and men lost their minds
In a rush to go northward and register finds
Yielding riches the timid man wouldn't achieve -
Lady Luck would be with him, each chose to believe.

Again, some would falter and then return where
They had first dreamed of riches in Gold lying there
To be grabbed for the promise of life without toil -
For them, such a dream had been destined to spoil.

For the first time away from the comforts of home,
Just the sight of a town such as Juno or Nome
From the deck of a boat caused such types to submit
To their fears and, of early defeat, to admit.

In the earth, in the streams, it was there for the taking.
One claim might yield big and the next end up making
　　Its owner a pauper – good fortune was rare
But, struck down by Gold Fever, a miner won't care.

And, from underground veins, at first dug out by hand,
There was Gold to be gotten, though in such demand
　　That the pick was replaced by the dynamite stick
And the dust in the mines hung on choking and thick.

　　But the call of the glittering Gold was so strong
That those who had heard it had run, right or wrong,
　　Each one following that irresistible call,
To find some would rise up but a great many fall.

Some would stumble and topple and then disappear
In the wastes and the wilds, and the ones they held dear
Would hear, never again, from the ones who embarked
On a dangerous quest when the passion was sparked.

But, like so many sheep with their eyes to the ground,
There was always a wolf on the prowl to be found
Which would strike at a weakness when on the attack,
Though a wolf, like a soldier, hunts best in a pack.

After months of hard toil, with a bagful of Gold,
　　There'd be many a miner beset by a bold
But despicable thief who would shoot the man dead
Leaving him short of Gold but abundant in Lead.

Even worse was the Government agent turned rogue.
And it seemed, to a miner, such things were in vogue
　　For he had to watch out for the greedy official
Who was often in league with the powers judicial.

A gauntlet was run past the Army deserters
Well armed; not to mention the money converters
Who'd swindle the miner each chance that he got -
He'd likely be fleeced just as likely as shot.

But some made it through, being wily enough
And, of course, being well armed and physically tough.
Some banded together to fight their way past
All the dangers they faced in a wilderness vast.

But the ones who made riches beyond all belief
Were the ones who provided much needed relief
From the tedium known to all those far from home
And would lose a year's earnings in one night in Nome.

Such a loser would often go back to his claims
Intent that, this time, he would stick to his aims
Of extracting a fortune by pick or by pan
And could go home in triumph, a very rich man.

But so many would give up and some would return
To their homes they had been all too eager to spurn
In a quest to grab riches beyond all belief –
Some would feel the disgrace and, some others, relief.

But the nature of things on the Earth would prevail –
There would always be someone prepared to assail
Someone else for his assets, deprive him of cash -
When a miner feels rich, he is bound to be rash.

The Arch-Fiend, Moriarty, had fingers in pies
Far away from his homeland – his sort never dies
Before stretching its network of criminal lust
To where gullible types look for someone to trust.

He set up his establishments, careful that he
Was kept well in the background - no way could he be
Linked to any wrongdoing – his agents were kept
At arm's length from a Master, at this, quite adept.

He did not have to send his men off robbing Gold
From the miners at diggings – his strategy bold
Was to get them to gamble their money away
While he'd rob any robbers who'd, too, come to play.

Moriarty sent agents to watch every house -
Every manager would act just as meek as a mouse
When it came to reporting the profit each made -
The wrath of the Master, one couldn't evade.

Anyone just suspected was guilty as charged.
There would be no appeal – those agents just barged
In and took to the party with hatchet and knife -
By means gruesome and public, he'd forfeit his life.

The public officials would all look away -
They were simply warned off or had been in the pay
Of a Master who had only one rule to state:
"Do what you are told or you'll suffer that fate."

To the Goldfields discovered all over the globe
Moriarty sent agents to survey and probe
Any means to divest anyone of his Gold -
Like a reptile, he watched them, his blood always cold.

But this cold-blooded reptile was cursed in his schemes
By the one who would thwart him and go to extremes
To reverse what he'd done and destroy what he'd built -
The Master of Crime would atone for his guilt.

And, atone, the man did, at the Reichenbach Falls
When he fell to his death at the base of those walls
Stretching up from the surge of the waters which swept
Moriarty away, though a secret it kept.

And that secret, of course, was that Sherlock survived -
He was hidden from view when John Watson arrived
At the scene of the struggle a little too late
And assumed Sherlock shared Moriarty's grim fate.

Although Watson went home, quite a figure forlorn,
Sherlock Holmes, in a sense, found he had been reborn
And, with help from his brother took no time to rest,
He'd make Moriarty's network his great quest.

That onerous quest lasted fully two years
Sherlock doing his utmost, although it appears
That not all of the network of crime was destroyed
Despite all of the methods Sherlock had employed.

Several men of significance to the grim Master
Avoided Sherlock and steered clear of disaster
Continuing on as they saw fit to do -
McIntyre and Murphy, to mention just two.

Though out in clear view, they could remain aloof
From the forces of Law due to absence of proof
They were linked to that fiend, Moriarty, departed
But alive in the plots and the schemes he had started.

They continued their schemes and continued to lift
Gold from gullible miners but they'd not the gift
Of Moriarty's networking, nor had they the urge -
They were well set up, therefore, to ride out the purge.

Sherlock would, in due time, reappear and retake
His position of old causing felons to shake
In their boots for they knew that, no matter the crime,
Sherlock Holmes would defeat them, it only took time.

With the Crime Lord defeated and dead and no longer
Controlling the dark streets of London, a stronger
Encouraging sense of law-biding arose
And, avoiding a criminal life, many chose.

Yet, all was not well – there were, though indistinct,
Several ominous signs which by luck and instinct
Were detected and recognised as an assault
To be made upon Britain. But who was at fault?

There was one who survived all the purges as he
Had been caught and imprisoned but found out to be
Out at liberty doing the things he desired -
Nobody knew with whom Moran had conspired.

But, conspire, the man had, and the clues led to Gold
After Sherlock, for months, had been out in the cold
And cut off from home-base, seemingly on his knees
On the South Downs of Sussex attending to bees.

Moriarty knew never to trust things to luck
And whatever his faults, the man simply had pluck
Complimenting the sense to keep well out of sight.
He was beaten, but after a long drawn-out fight.

His able Lieutenant, a Colonel long since,
Was as good as his Master, himself he'd convince.
Moriarty left details of one daring plan -
With that Master now dead, it passed on to Moran.

In his unstable mind, he desired a crown
And assumed Britain's Empire would come crashing down
Although he'd, in due course, learn a lesson quite bitter -
He had Gold in sight but was blinded by glitter.

THE DECEIVERS

Three days would elapse till the pair crossed the bay
So that, on their long journey, they could be away
Heading off to embark on a dangerous quest -
The banks of Great Britain, of Gold, to divest.

They did not know all details but knew that the plan
Would be one of deception – they knew that Moran
Would attack Britain's Gold, that supporting the Pound,
So that Britain's elite would all come crashing down.

They would share in the spoils and have so much Gold
And the Pound would be worthless – it was such a bold
And audacious endeavour – they couldn't see past
All the glitter of Gold onto misery vast.

That the masses would suffer would cause no regret -
Murphy had come on board for all that he could get
While McIntyre wanted revenge and the power
To get those who'd crossed him to grovel and cower.

Neither one knew the plan called for war to be waged
On a scale unimaginable and, while it raged,
They would wait with Moran and their ill-gotten Gold
Till they could with their riches, of Europe, take hold.

Had they known of this fact, they'd have realised Moran
Had gone mad and was trying to outdo the man
Who he knew as his Master. They would have, instead
Of becoming involved, simply shot Moran dead.

They did not need a world which was ruined so badly
That no one could win – but they blundered on, sadly,
Awaiting the chance for the Pound to be tumbled -
Murphy's riches enhanced, Mack's tormentors humbled.

They had little in common, both Murphy and Mack,
Although each one possessed what the other might lack
For, while Murphy was stable. not prone to distraction,
McIntyre was wild, always ready for action.

Though incredibly different in makeup and manner,
They'd both undertaken to hold up the banner
Moran handed to them – they both had sworn true -
To go back on his word, neither was of the hue.

Though corrupt, each had honour, at least of a sort,
But of scruples and conscience, each one would fall short
When it came to the misery they might impart
When, Moran's plan of action, they'd finally start.

As the guard called for boarding, the whistle blew loud
And the steam from the engine resembled a cloud
And the pair settled in for a long bumpy ride
On America's high Rocky Mountain divide.

From the very first moment their journey commenced
Murphy had felt uncomfortable, McIntyre fenced
Once again in a box which just wouldn't keep still,
And this when encountering only a hill.

They'd be constantly jostled as they went ascending
The Rockies – the train would be constantly bending
This way and then that as each corner was rounded -
Ideas of a leisurely trip were unfounded.

McIntyre was still overcoming the strain
Of his long schooner voyage – at times he'd complain
But would find little sympathy coming his way -
Murphy, on discomfort, had little to say.

At last, past the summit, the going got easy -
McIntyre, for one, felt a little less queasy
And hoped for a gentle enjoyable ride,
At least one as tranquil as trains might provide.

Days of travel would pass relieved only by stops
For passengers, water and fuel, where one hops
To the unmoving ground, stretching, hoping to gain
A renewed sense of balance, then back on the train.

Further east, the pace slackened, new towns testified
To a burgeoning nation, one intensified
By its industry spreading westward filling space
At what seemed to the pair an unstoppable pace.

Onward past Chicago, across the heartland
Of American enterprise filling demand
From the west and the east, overseas and within -
McIntyre watched Murphy conceal a grin.

He had money to burn, but in Dollars not Pounds,
And looked forward to getting his share of the mounds
Of Gold taken from bankers – just fools, he had thought -
He saw them as weaklings – their riches, he sought.

McIntyre wanted money, and property, too,
And was, as Murphy said, like a wild kangaroo
At times jumping at problems that didn't exist -
To be useful, that urge, he would have to resist.

McIntyre couldn't understand Murphy's reserve.
He did not even know if the man had the nerve
To stand up in a fight and do battle and win -
He did not know what Murphy held under his skin.

That the man could be ruthless, he knew to be true
But, for doing the dirty work, hadn't a clue
If the man was up to it. So, could the man fight
If he had to? Maybe no, but then he just might.

Murphy, too, was uncertain on what to expect.
Was it madness in McIntyre he could detect
Or an immature trait to fulfil a desire
To dress up in his uniform, playing the Squire?

They would both have to keep level heads to succeed
In whatever Moran had in play – each would need
To rely on the other. But could this be done?
Could each man rely fully on that other one?

At New York, having travelled a whole week together,
They still had to face a great ocean, and whether
They might remain allies with mutual trust
Couldn't be guaranteed – the whole thing could go bust.

Half a week they would pass, distrust unmitigated;
Murphy, ever the pragmatist, anticipated
The break-up of any alliance, and suggested
The two of them get all such problems divested.

"We are quite different men, you and I," Murphy stated,
"And it seems, on our differences we are fixated.
I suggest there is more within each to detect -
We might have more in common than we might suspect."

"I am not a campaigner, my skills keep me bound
To a desk and an office, though sometimes I'm found
Facing down wayward types when I need to be tough -
It has been more than once that I've had to get rough."

"I see you as the soldier – a man born to fight
And, in winning each battle, take greatest delight.
I admit I don't like to take risks of that sort -
I will fight when I have to, not simply for sport."

"But I would never leave you to battle alone -
That is something which even I wouldn't condone.
But my skills are in details, in keeping the books,
And I learned long ago not to judge men by looks."

"I like cheating at cards, just for sport, you should know;
If you deal me five cards I'll be able to show
You an Ace or a colour card at every turn -
Thoughts of beating me at the card table, I'd spurn."

"Perhaps, on our voyage across the Atlantic,
We might pair up to drive every gambler frantic
By taking his money - after all, that's our game -
Missing out on the prospect would be a great shame."

"It'll help pass the time and we might come to see
One-another as comrades who have to agree
That the best sport of all is in scooping the pool
Taking everything off every gambling fool."

"With our accents so different, we won't be suspected.
Our card table antics will not be detected
And if we agree to appear to be strangers,
We won't come across as a pair of bushrangers."

"We would not be strung up but it's possible that
We'd be thrown overboard and a very loud 'splat'
Would be all that was heard as we hit the Atlantic -
A very wet end to our mischievous antic."

McIntyre gave a laugh saying, *"That's what we'll do.*
Though I did have misgivings, I'm warming to you
As a comrade in cards – I'll take care of the arms.
I admit I'm succumbing to your wily charms."

Two tickets to sail had been ordered by wire
And were picked up directly. The pair would retire
Into different lodgings – their ruse would unravel
If noticed together before they could travel.

On the day they would sail, they separately made
Their own ways to the docks having separately bade
A farewell to America as they embarked -
The cards they would use had already been marked.

McIntyre went on incognito as he
Had been registered as M. McBride and as he,
As a wanted deserter, might be recognised
And the British authorities duly advised.

So it fell to his colleague, Murphy, to be seated
Without McIntyre, just a little defeated,
To dine with the Captain and ten chosen few -
Mack joked that he'd rather dine out with the crew.

This would fit, rather well, with their gambling plan -
Murphy now would appear as trustworthy man
Having dined with the Captain – this man wouldn't cheat
And for some little time he'd be easy to beat.

As the evening wore on, he would increase his bets
Till the pot was as big as gambling house lets
And then, little by little, he'd win more and more
Taking care to lose sometimes while keeping the score.

McIntyre waited patiently, biding his time
Till he sensed that there was opportunity prime
As a player would fold and rise up from the table -
The pair would fleece all of what they would be able.

McIntyre would beat Murphy and then boast and brag
That he'd have to go fetching a much bigger bag
That would hold all his winnings – he played his part well
And, of their being cheated, the rest couldn't tell.

Murphy then would retire up to the saloon
Where he sat talking finance like some great tycoon
Knowing well that his comrade was counting the loot
In his cabin below having played the galloot.

Murphy would be sought out as a gentleman, true,
While most saw McIntyre in a different hue.
It was quite a good game, they were having great fun
Catching flies in the gambling web they had spun.

They did not win too much – they took care to lose most
Of the hands that they played, even more care to host
A selection of after-game drinks at the bar -
This game that they played could be taken too far.

They enjoyed their deception, it gave them the chance
To get used to each other and then to advance
To whatever Moran had prepared in regards
Of a much greater gamble than Murphy's marked cards.

Two weeks on board ship and the pair sometimes met
Over drinks in the bar, sometimes making a bet
That someone could be conned, or perhaps maybe not,
Taking care not to seem as if hatching a plot.

At last, at Southampton, the pair disembarked
And discovered Moran had a four-wheeler parked
At the docks so they all could transfer in good time
To a train bound for London to prepare the crime.

They would travel in silence and not give a sign
They were planning a great operation, malign.
That evening they'd dine, they would rest for one night
Then they meet with Moran to discuss Britain's plight.

They were told Sherlock Holmes was a force truly spent
And, to look after bees down in Sussex was sent
Then returned fully broken in spirit and drive -
If he once interfered, he would not stay alive.

But a taunt had been sent and this kept him at bay -
He would not be the danger he was in his day
And had fled to his chambers and barred all its doors -
He was still too afraid of the beast of the moors.

Moran didn't tell of the messages sent
To provoke a great war – there was simply the scent
Of a quarry to follow, a fortune to steal -
The pair should have recognised such a bad deal.

Did they truly think Britain would fall for the trick?
Any move on the Pound must result in a quick
And quite robust response in a manner untold.
Or had they been blinded by glittering Gold?

Or did they expect there was more to the plan?
If they had to trust someone, it would be Moran.
They thought on the great power that might be received -
Could it be these deceivers became the deceived?

THE MOVE

In London, Moran was deploying his men
So a move could be made on the Gold bullion when
The banks made the decision to transfer their Gold
Somewhere out of the city, to some secure hold.

It would be to the north - that much they all knew -
But the Gold's destination was known to just few.
Moran knew that it had to all travel by rail -
He had matters prepared and felt he couldn't fail.

He knew well there were special trains waiting to load
At the Marylebone Station but, coming by road
Would be wagons of Gold plodding slowly along
London's streets – to attack any here would be wrong.

No attacker would have any hope of escape -
Laden down, he'd have no hope of winning a scrape
With an able policeman – thus had thought Moran
So, hijacking the train became part of the plan.

This must be out of London, from where a train might
Be diverted to somewhere, in cold dead of night,
And the Gold could be transferred in bulk to a ship
Which then, over to some foreign country, would slip.

Moran had his lieutenants to stand by his side -
McIntyre and Murphy were types who'd provide
Full support for his vision – he had explained all
Except that he would need all of Europe to fall.

He needed them both to set up his empire
And had said to them both that each one might aspire
To have riches and power beyond all belief
When the nations of Europe had all come to grief.

His words sounded lucid but, in fact, below
The facade he created, he'd little to show
Beyond being a nuisance, albeit quite large -
He just wanted to sound like the big man in charge.

At the end of his discourse on trains bearing Gold
He would tell them the rest of his plan, far too bold
And outrageous for others to bring into play -
"War," Moran told them, *"might start any day."*

He would tell of his plans for a conflict, full-blown,
To descend over Europe, and when that was known,
The pair stared at each other in stark disbelief -
Each one had considered Moran just a thief.

Now it seemed to them both he was reaching for stars
Seeking lands dominated by Princes and Czars
And defended by armies all poised to attack
But also, it seemed, there was no turning back.

However, the war would not come to fruition.
By fate and by fortune and great intuition,
The fuse Moran lit to set Europe alight
Fizzled out, though it gave some a terrible fright.

He'd sent counterfeit documents hoping to trigger
A war between nations, a war so much bigger
Than any before. When this plot was defused
It left Whitehall alerted and most unamused.

With assistance from Watson and Holmes and the Tower,
Whitehall used its diplomacy and all its power
And brought Moran's dreams down to earth with a thud
When his pretexts for war were all nipped in the bud.

Moran, of course, didn't know that he'd been foiled -
His plans for a war had been utterly spoiled
By those forces he ought to have known would respond
To a threat to Great Britain and nations beyond.

He did not know the Gold to be moved was, instead
Of being bank-secured bullion, just Gold-painted Lead
In a counter plot set up to draw out the man
And his cohorts, defusing the rest of the plan.

He continued as though there'd be Gold on the rail
Which he'd divert to Grimsby, determined to sail
To the Dutch port of Rotterdam loaded with Gold,
So he thought, deeply hidden within the ship's hold.

And, if all progressed well, the Gold would be unloaded
On barges which then, through canals, would be goaded
Then sunk in the shallows – Gold would be retrieved
Once, the crown of all Europe, Moran had received.

His delusions were nonsense, great folly at best;
Foolish dreams of a mind which was once full of zest
For the hunt, for adventure, for playing with danger -
With his master destroyed, his thoughts became stranger.

McIntyre and Murphy thought him quite detached
From reality over this plan he had hatched;
They did not want a war of such tremendous scope
But, of coming home rich, had expressed a great hope.

Now, on being informed of the plot to ignite
A great war across Europe, the pair would unite
In a plan of their own to despatch mad Moran,
Carry on with the heist, get away if they can.

So, over to Rotterdam, McIntyre sailed
With Moran to have the ship's captain availed
Of procedures and timing and what to expect -
Their instructions, explicit and very direct.

McIntyre felt things weren't exactly quite right
For he feared the ship's Captain, to some others, might
Just have mentioned the cargo as being his own -
McIntyre would have such a scheme overthrown.

He knew some Afrikaans which would double for Dutch
And he thought that the Captain had said he would clutch
Any prospect for profit which might come his way,
Any cargo which might, to his ownership, stray.

But he could not be sure – it was quite hard to tell
What the Captain had actually said. Should he quell
His suspicions of being sold out for a price?
He should act, he believed, on his own good advice.

So he thought if the plan went completely awry
He would like to escape and emerge high and dry
With no way to be traced – he'd be free and away
To continue his antics on some later day.

So he said to Moran that there needed to be
No link back to himself nor to any that he
Had entrusted with setting the plan into motion -
Moran thought long and hard on this troubling notion.

McIntyre knew that the ship's Captain was told
Of a difficult cargo, but not of the Gold.
He'd have sealed instructions locked soundly away
To be opened and read when the game was in play.

He suggested the ship might be blown right apart
Should the plan, in some manner, unravel and start
To go horribly wrong – he just needed to find
Quantities of explosives of just the right kind.

Dynamite was obtainable readily for
Such a man as Moran – and a detonator
Could be readily rigged, McIntyre expressed,
Just in case things went bad as their caper progressed.

Two days later, the pair had returned to the ship
Which was, into the harbour, required to slip;
Time was now running short – the bomb had to be set -
McIntyre, however, was not one to fret.

Several chests of equipment, on dinghies, were towed
And transferred to the ship and then carefully stowed.
They would both stay on board for the night and depart
From the ship in the morning, one hour apart.

The pair dined with the Captain and quickly retired
To the Second Mate's cabin where McIntyre wired
. Up a trigger to counter a possible threat
Causing Colonel Moran to break out in a sweat.

He had two chests of dynamite carefully placed
Deep down inside the ship, with a long wire traced
To the Second Mate's cabin, by him occupied -
It would blow the ship skyward with current applied.

To a chest in that cabin, he'd rigged up the wire
So the detonator for the bomb would acquire
Enough tension to cause a taut switch to be thrown
And the bomb, and the boat, into bits, to be blown.

All the notes held within with detailed instruction,
Would just disappear in the utter destruction
Set off if somebody tried lifting the chest
And would, to the sea, all its contents, divest.

The chest would be locked till the time came to read
All within and the Captain could then take his lead.
But the ship and the chest and details of the plot,
McIntyre, to allow being taken, would not.

He had done this before, on the Veldt, booby trapping
The haunts of the Boers with whom he'd been scrapping.
Sometimes he'd use batteries or, sometimes, a wick
Would be set to be lit, though he'd have to be quick.

He preferred to use batteries to fire detonators
Though they did require skilful and calm operators
To set up the wiring and trigger device
For, to blow oneself up, would be too high a price.

With electrical circuits, he learned that he could
Keep his distance from targets – as much as he should.
There was never a bomb the man could not devise -
It there was one thing he could do, it was improvise.

Though he did prefer combat and meet face to face
With an enemy, worthy, he had to embrace
Any method which would bring the enemy down -
For no-holds-barred fighting, the man was renown.

The Captain would be told, upon reaching the dock
In the harbour of Grimsby, the key to the lock
Of the chest would be handed to him so he could
Take instruction of where to proceed that he should.

But if ever, at sea, he'd be challenged and stopped
By the Naval Command, the chest had to be dropped
Overboard without fail, else its contents would hang
Everybody aboard with Moran and his gang.

But at Grimsby, somebody would sever the wire
To render the bomb quite unable to fire
And detonate with such incredible might
That the fate of the thieves never could come to light.

Once the bomb was in place and the trigger deployed,
McIntyre to Moran said, *"I've always enjoyed
Your support and your company but I contend
That to cause war in Europe is madness, My Friend."*

Before any response could be heard from Moran,
McIntyre had taken the life of the man
Who had given him much and had promised him more -
A blade, keen and fast, was soon covered in gore.

With the body then hidden away in the hold
Of the ship, McIntyre's thoughts all turned to Gold
As he slept like a baby, the game underway -
Moran's mind-numbing madness, the man could allay.

The next morning he said that, while all was still dark,
Moran had decided he would disembark
Before McIntyre did – all the beacons were bright.
McIntyre had rowed him ashore before light.

McIntyre then took leave of the Captain and rowed
To the shore thinking of the great seed that he sowed.
Then he scurried to London where boxes of Lead
Would be off to the rail at a good steady tread.

Two great plans were in action, one poised to fall short
Of its great expectations – the Government rort
Left them little of worth even if it succeeded;
The other plan, silence and planning, had needed.

Just in time, McIntyre returned to be told
There was movement afoot and the word was that Gold
Would be moved from the banks on that very same night -
He received the good tidings with utter delight.

McIntyre and Murphy, to Grimsby, transferred
There to meet up with Percy the Ponce who deferred
To them both as his masters – all things were prepared -
The trap had been set and the prey would be snared.

Slowly, slowly, the wagons of Jackson advanced
From the banks to the railway, always with the chance
Of attack, although small – still, all were quite prepared
For a fight just in case any plotters had dared.

As the Gold-painted Lead was transferred to the train,
Holmes and others hid with it and had to refrain
From all talking – no chance of detection they'd risk -
The night dragged along at a pace never brisk.

At last, off and away, heading North, a train cleared
The new Marylebone station, while silently cheered
By all those who had waited in silence, all cramped,
As impatient as horses with bits being champed.

Then train number two, in due course, followed on
Past the first of the many checkpoints, whereupon
A short message was telegraphed further ahead
To signal *"All's well."* or *"There's trouble."* instead.

Before reaching Sheffield, the first train would divert
To the east and, before anyone could alert
The authorities, the second would follow along
Unaware for some time that the plan had gone wrong.

But, of course, this diversion was always expected
And Grimsby and Hull had been duly selected
As locations likely if Gold would be sent
To somewhere on the coast of the great Continent.

In both these locations the Army was ready
And poised to attack - ever vigilant, steady
In ranks under orders to hide as demanded
Then charge on the foe when their Captain commanded.

It was Grimsby, the Docks, which Moran had decided
Was best for a ship which would need to be guided
To shores, quite unknown, under cover of dark -
Hull was too complicated to stage such a lark.

The first train would arrive and, on board with the Gold,
Was a rabble of sailors, all used to the cold
And the hard heavy work they were paid well to do -
They all milled around unsure just who was who.

Then a shout came from Percy, *"Break off all the locks*
And we'll get the train moving on down to the docks.
The second train's coming – come on, move your feet.
The Sun will soon rise and its face we shan't meet."

With the second train halted, the sailors all bristled -
Captain Roberts had signalled his men with a whistle
And three ranks of bayonets flashed brightly as flares
Lit the rail yards up catching all unawares.

Resistance was feeble, almost every arm
Was raised up overhead as contagious alarm
Had spread throughout the rabble – some tried to escape
But John Watson proved he was in much better shape.

His old Army revolver was pointed and steady
To fire – John Watson, the soldier, was ready
To shoot if he had to, to die if he must,
But the escapees' courage turned, quickly, to dust.

Murphy, down on the docks, had looked on as the rout
Took its course and the soldiers formed ranks all about
What to him had appeared a ridiculous lot
Who'd been beaten by troops hardly firing a shot.

As he tried to stay hidden, their ship would appear
Looking out for the signal which said it was near
Grimsby Docks. But it turned as a Naval gunboat
Called upon it to stop or expect not to float.

A shot sent as a warning went soaring above
And the Captain, to get to Moran's chest, would shove
Everyone in his way and, as he gave a pull
On the chest, an explosion came sudden and full.

Murphy scrambled for cover as all eyes were fixed
To the blast on the water – his options were mixed.
Moriarty was dead, McIntyre perhaps taken -
The whole escapade had left Murphy quite shaken.

He had cash in his pocket and more stashed away
Back in London to use upon some later day.
But that day had now come – it was time to retreat -
It would be a wise man who would accept defeat.

He would creep back to London, his funds to retrieve,
Before leaving forever – he couldn't believe
He'd been duped by a madman and left on the docks,
Alone and defenceless, a shag on the rocks.

In defeat, Murphy wrote a few words on a note
To be carried to Sherlock – it carried a vote
Of approval for one who was first in his craft -
He admired this man never bitten by graft.

It would briefly declare that the threat Britain faced
Was defused, while implying it had been replaced
By a strengthening peace, though he didn't say so -
He just signed it with 'M' – it was then time to go.

He then hastened to board the first ship he could find.
Where it went to, this 'M', the least bit, didn't mind.
He would make his way back to his home to lay low -
For his Golden adventure, he'd nothing to show.

But he was still alive with funds more than enough
To return home in style – his life wouldn't be tough
But would be a lot better for loss of Moran -
From now on, he determined to be his own man.

McIntyre escaped from the Grimsby yard rout
Quite disgusted with those who gave up with the shout
Of *"Don't shoot, we surrender"* with nary a shot
Being fired – McIntyre detested the lot.

He'd jumped into a ditch and kept perfectly still,
His face down in the mud and the rubbish until
He detected no sound, then emerged wet and soiled
Wondering how he might get, in a new fight, embroiled.

No one knew who he was except Murphy who'd just
Disappeared from the face of the earth and who must
Be considered a casualty of the plan
Instigated in folly by Colonel Moran.

McIntyre, alone, knew the fate of Moran
Who went down with the ship as it took every man
As it sunk on exploding – no one could he tell -
So he stay as McBride which he thought just as well.

Then, while Murphy escaped as the unknown man
And the ship had exploded and taken Moran
To a watery grave, never more to be seen,
McIntyre planned vengeance on Empire and Queen.

He felt safe for the moment - no one, he presumed,
Would know of his identity, real or assumed.
But, purely by chance, there'd be put into play
A search for the subject of Watson's hearsay.

THE ASSEMBLY

As the Knights of the Tower arrived and assembled
At Andre's establishment, they had resembled
A hotch-potch of visitors, acting unknown
To each other, of course, with no interest shown.

In small groups and in pairs and at times quite alone,
They ascended the stairs with a dull monotone
Of discussions of nothing, just words being muttered
Without any sense of intent being uttered.

As each took a seat at the table, Holmes sought
To sit next to his friend for he felt that he ought
To show all there that evening he'd always be there
For Watson, his colleague and friend, anywhere.

Denton started things off with a call to take seats
And select, from a menu of delicious treats,
Any preference held from the restaurant's fare
Though most took that provided, its taste, full aware.

There had been no discussion of matters selected
By any attendee – each one was elected
For character strength, for the resolve to keep
Any matters to bring up within oneself, deep.

The meals were delivered and quickly despatched
And then coffee was poured and the door firmly latched
To prevent any ears, uninvited, from hearing
The matters which troubled attendees were fearing.

Porter stood, tapped his glass and said, *"Now we begin*
With discussions of matters which should stay within
Our discrete dinner group till we all can decide
What and how and to whom, tonight's work, to provide."

"We're aware of events which negated a move
To divert lots of Gold bars, a move which would prove
To be foolish and dangerous at the same time -
A move made of treason and also of crime."

"The Newspapers are mute upon some of the facts.
They know well that a wrong word unduly impacts
Upon delicate matters of murderous men -
Even they see the need to pull back now and then."

"The truth may come out in due course but, by then,
Any danger engendered won't matter. So when
The news breaks it will seem to be news of the past
And the worry the Public may feel will not last."

"Mr Holmes has informed me of lingering fears
He holds of those events for, to him, it appears
There was more to the matter than he at first thought
And our Tower, to meet and discuss things, now ought."

Sherlock rose to address all those at the Round Table:
"Though to give all the facts at this time, I'm unable,
I have now, as before, been delivered a note
I had thought from my brother – one he never wrote."

"It made mention of threats to our nation being foiled,
Threats to get it with some others embroiled
In a war of a size which had never been fought -
It was signed just with 'M', 'M' for 'Mycroft' I thought."

"But that note wasn't written by Mycroft, my brother,
It was written and despatched by somebody other
Than he, but someone who knew well I would find
It was false – someone who had mischief in mind."

"I say mischief, but that could mean murder for one
Or for millions, My Friends, if we hadn't undone
The devices that evil had planned to deploy -
I don't know what 'M' wants. It might be a decoy."

"Of those in this room, I would ask if they know
Or have heard or have seen or have something to show
Which might point to a clue about who may have sent
Me that note – is there something we need to prevent?"

A few of the members uncomfortably shuffled
A little and, then, came a cough and a muffled
Response of , *"Well Sherlock, that is, My Dear Friends,*
I have something and ask what our group recommends."

Somewhat nervous, John Watson spoke up as per plan,
"Upon this very morning I talked with a man
Who related a tale about African Gold
And a shiver went through me and left me quite cold."

"I've sense," declared Watson, *"of things left undone*
From the 'M' of that note and a tale of one
Wayward military man, a colonial fellow,
Whose acts are described as a long way from mellow."

"I've a name to put to him, this military chap -
McIntyre from Melbourne, someone who can tap
Into personal courage of conscience devoid -
A fellow who many would choose to avoid."

97

"He's an officer, so I was given to hear,
And a very brave man, so it seems to appear.
His men, so I'm told, would all follow him willing
To die right beside him or keep right on killing."

"His daring is reckless, his chivalry, nought,
But he does have that instinct that great leaders ought
To display when surrounded, unnumbered, outflanked -
And for many a victory he must be thanked."

"But I'm saying too much – I am going too far
Telling more than I know but he does seem on par
With another ex-soldier, one Colonel Moran,
And might well be the type to fall in with the man."

"I haven't discussed this with Holmes, as requested.
I bring facts before you so they can be tested
For sense and veracity, logic or lie,
And if any more facts, into this tale, tie."

"That's no slight upon Sherlock - the man I've not seen
For a day, maybe more. Not a word's passed between
Us on what I have heard on a short morning's jaunt -
If these fact come to nothing, they certainly taunt."

Watson sat, feeling awkward but also relieved
That he had done his duty – he hoped all believed
He'd been earnest with what he felt he must disclose.
Intrigued, Dr Denton, from sitting, arose.

"If they cause you discomfort, Watson, then I'd say
That they need looking into without much delay.
Anything which unsettles the mind, we must check."
Said Denton, *"The man may have plans we must wreck."*

"Have you more you may tell us? If so, Watson, do
For I'm certain that all 'round this table wish to
Know whatever it is that has got you perturbed -
What is it, exactly, that got you disturbed."

Watson stood, coughed a little, adjusted his tie,
Looked around as if he was refuting a lie.
Sherlock then gave him one of his *"get to it"* looks
Saying *"Speak up, now, Watson. We're on tenterhooks."*

"Well, I'd say," Watson uttered, his voice hesitating,
And, just how to render his tale, contemplating,
"It was how the discussion commenced and expanded
Without help from me or its being demanded."

"I say 'no help from me', though I did help a little
By acting as though I had hours to whittle
Away – and stallholders love telling a story
Especially so if the subject is gory."

"It was something about the man's manner, you see.
I was unknown to him, though his story came free
And entirely unhindered – no one could have known
I was trawling for what I might hear or be shown."

"As if taking the air, I just happened to stroll
To the markets where I had a few rather droll
And amusing exchanges – those men like to talk -
And with what one man told me, I finished my walk."

"I completed my purchases, saying my life
Would be made quite a misery by my good wife
If I didn't return with some treats for our table -
Though those who know Mary, know that is a fable."

"I returned to my home to make notes for tonight,
For our dinner, that is, where between us we might
Make some sense of the matter of 'M' and this man
Who seems more of a menace than Colonel Moran."

"I know nothing, of course, of the man or if he
Even truly exists – but it does seem to me
A most curious matter when letters are signed
Simply 'M'. Has the man, with Moran, been aligned?"

"He had been a Lieutenant, or so went the story,
And perhaps for adventure and maybe for glory
Sailed off to fight Boers which he did rather well
With irregular forces the Boers couldn't quell."

"The stall-holder said friends all addressed him as Mick
But his troops called him Mack which he got as a nick
Name - short for McIntyre – that's his information.
He was made Brevet Major, just for the duration."

"But I must press the point that what I had been told
Started out as a discourse on food then on Gold
In an innocent way with no mention of fighting
In Africa or places more uninviting."

"That stallholder's a stranger, I do not frequent
That particular market – at random, I went
Down one street then another – nobody could know,
Even me, where I'd drift when the wind chose to blow."

"His cousin, it seems, out in Africa fought
With Colonial troops who were favourably sought
For their prowess with small arms and horses and could
Live quite well off the land and undoubtedly would."

"There's no more I can tell you, none I can recall
At this moment, but I have to say to you all
That a shiver went charging the length of my spine -
To declare it all hearsay, I'd have to decline."

"It is quite a coincidence, you would agree
That a stranger would be so incredibly free
With such detail which meshes with recent events
Were it not for our need of a few more fresh scents."

"A coincidence, possibly; maybe a clue
Which we may be advised to discuss and pursue."
Declared Denton, intrigued, though prepared to admit
That there might just be lots of hot air behind it.

"Can I ask for a comment from those seated here?
Do we follow this up or declare it a mere
Tale tall being told by a vendor of fruit?
Or do we," Denton added, *"charge off in pursuit?"*

"We should first ascertain if this soldier exists.
If he does, he'll be on the Colonial lists.
Though commissioned in battle, it would be confirmed."
Said Porter who had, at the very thought, squirmed.

"His record of service might be summarised.
Although, on active duty, we might be advised
To have someone of rank or authority seek
Out the answers we need, or at least have a peek."

"If the fruit vendor's stories turn out to be lies
We might all be arrested for being Boer spies."
Mrs Tully said, worried that they might be sent
To a cell, dark and damp, which she'd like to prevent.

"What about Sherlock's brother, that man in Whitehall
Or where-ever he works? Could we pay him a call
And get him to ask questions? He'd surely be able
To look the man up on some military table."

"To ask questions of Mycroft, we may be quite free,
But, of getting replies, there is no guarantee."
Sherlock said with a chuckle, well knowing his brother
Might listen to him though he would to no other.

He knew also the leaders of Government ranks
Beg indulgence of Mycroft and always give thanks
For a man with a mind which can process and hold
Information on people when troubles unfold.

"If our group so directs, I will visit Mycroft
In his home or, perhaps, in his office aloft
In that edifice, noble, and ask if he might
Help us out. It depends on what's said here tonight."

"I just cannot turn up asking questions like that
For, although he's my brother, he'll think I'm a brat
Interfering in matters I don't understand.
To have something of substance, the man will demand."

"There, of course, is that matter of 'M' on that note
Which, to me, meant my brother, though did not denote
'Mycroft' as I had thought. So he might feel disposed
To do me a small favour, it might be supposed."

"Watson's talk with the vendor's intriguing, indeed,
And I'd like to go further but think that we need
Just a little more data, perhaps one more hint,
To have both Mycroft's eyes show an interested glint."

Lady Margaret said, *"Well, if I may be so bold,*
My husband, Sir Humphrey, went out on a cold
And quite miserable morning on some urgent quest -
I think that he said he was heading out west."

"Well, I think he said 'west' but I may have been wrong
For it was to some officer tagging along
As they hopped in the carriage which took them away
And I've not seen my husband for more than a day."

"Two days and one night, if I must be correct,
Although where he was headed, I couldn't detect,
But I'm sure he said 'west' and the rest was all muffled
As, into the carriage, the pair of them shuffled."

"He went off and I haven't had word from him since
And the thoughts in my mind only cause me to wince.
I expect that I'll hear from my husband quite soon -
As far as I know, he could be on the moon."

"On the moon, way out west – that just isn't much help -
He might be in west Ireland gathering kelp
Or perhaps in Westminster attending to chores,"
Said Sherlock, *"with sweat oozing out of his pores."*

"Well, now who's unhelpful?" the Lady replied,
"Dr Watson told us what he heard when he tried
To find out what he could – I am doing the same
And I do feel your comment was really quite lame."

"Lady Margaret, forgive me, I pondered out loud
But I meant no offence to your husband whose proud
And esteemed reputation should not be maligned."
Sherlock quickly responded, *"To help, I'm resigned."*

"But the critical fact is Sir Humphrey has left,
Very quickly it seems, and it's left you bereft
Of that peace of mind needed to say there exists
Nothing worthy of worry – your anguish persists."

No more facts were forthcoming and so Porter rose
Saying that the proceedings would come to a close
After getting consensus from those who attended -
Sherlock would see Mycroft, it was recommended.

Sherlock said he would meet with his brother as soon
As he could – in the morning, perhaps, afternoon.
He would hope that a conference could be arranged,
But the world, as they knew it, was set to be changed.

THE KING

In the midst of a war, having one year to run,
Empire against Boer, man to man, gun to gun,
Loyal people were shaken – the news was quite bad
And, though not unexpected, appallingly sad.

An outpouring of grief started slowly, then spread
As the rumours went coursing, always far ahead
Of official announcements – *"No. No-one had lied -*
Victoria, our Queen and our Empress has died."

Crowds formed at the Palace – in thousands they milled;
From their homes and workplaces they rapidly spilled
Seeking word from officials who, when they appeared,
Would confirm the sad tidings which everyone feared.

The streets were all filled with cacophonous yells
And the churches were tolling the saddest of bells;
Every flag was descending halfway down its pole;
Total strangers, each other, would stop to console.

Word reached Baker Street as the bells began ringing
And poor Mrs Hudson at once started flinging
Her shopping aside as she rushed to relate,
To her tenant, the news of Victoria's fate.

He had been contemplating the way he might broach
Urgent matters with Mycroft, meanwhile a coach
Had been ordered but seemed to be running quite late.
Just as well – he must bow to the needs of the State.

Any carriage, of course, would be hard pressed to drive
Through the crowds in the streets – it would never arrive
In good time to take Sherlock to where he'd be told
That his meeting was off and his tongue he must hold.

On his door, Mrs Hudson was banging her fist
In a manner determined - she wouldn't desist
Saying something quite awful had just been announced
And, as Sherlock appeared in the doorway, she pounced.

Mrs Hudson charged in just as fast as she could,
In fact more than Sherlock considered she should.
But she wouldn't be stopped – she had news to deliver
And no sooner was in than she said with a shiver:

*"It's bad news, Mr Holmes, for the Old Queen is dead
And Prince Eddie, we're told, is to reign in her stead.
He's an old man himself – we don't know if he'll last
Or if he is quite up to the role he's been cast."*

"Did you not hear the bells ringing throughout the city?
They're all mournful and sad, ringing sorrow and pity
For the loss we have suffered this terrible day.
I think the whole nation has now lost its way."

Sherlock heard Mrs Hudson pound hard on the door
But continued to pace back and forth on the floor
Till she pounded so hard that he had to relent
And release the door latch, for his focus was spent.

Holmes hadn't answered for some little time.
There were matters afoot to which he would give prime
And complete concentration – he needed to sort
Matters out in his mind – time might be running short.

It was not long ago that Sherlock had been called
To return to the Moors when some killings appalled
All the folks in the district and Timothy Jones
Had declared all were terrified down to their bones.

Holmes, Watson at hand, solved the mystery but,
He was told quite explicitly, *"Keep your mouth shut."*
On his theory that some unidentified party
Was none other than he, the deceased Moriarty.

Great anxiety followed and Holmes would retreat
To raise bees down in Sussex till folks would entreat
His return back to London, but there he would stumble
Across such a plot which might make Britain crumble.

Threats to Gold in the vaults of the banks of the nation
Had been causing those high in the land trepidation;
Also mischievous types sought to bring to fruition
A war with those jealous of Britain's position.

These were found to be linked, in a curious way,
To events on the Moors which were put into play
By the actions of Colonel Moran, it was thought,
Although further details would need to be sought.

And with what Watson told to the Tower, he saw
That, though war was averted, one act might well draw
Out the Kaiser and place him where he couldn't back
Off supporting the Boers – he might choose to attack.

Mrs Hudson, however, gave out a great yelp,
Unconcerned for the Kaiser and who he might help.
The Queen she had known for the whole of her life
Was now gone and the rumours of chaos were rife.

"Yes, indeed, Mrs Hudson. It has come, I fear,
That the reign of that old gracious Queen we hold dear
Has now come to its end." Sherlock stated, aware
The new King would have had ample time to prepare.

"The Crown prince will ascend to his duties this day.
That has been the tradition and will be the way
Continuity's kept for the head of our nation -
We will hold, in due time, the King's grand coronation."

Sherlock knew well, however, those family links
Long kept up by the Queen were displaying great chinks
As the Great Chain of Monarchs was turning to rust -
They had things still to bind them, but one wasn't trust.

With the war in South Africa taking too long
And so many insisting her methods were wrong,
Britain knew that the Kaiser's impatience was showing -
His sabres were rattling, his bugles were blowing.

There were calls for support for the Boers to be given.
This might lead to Britain's ambitions being driven
Away to a point at which war couldn't be
Long avoided in Europe - then catastrophe.

It would be the King's lot to seek acts diplomatic -
He could not act alone, he was not autocratic
But bound by constitution – the Parliament must
By a time-honoured process, bring peace, fast and just.

But *"Push hard!"* was the word, *"We want this job done.*
Wars are never the noble things which anyone
Who has ever confronted adversaries, armed,
Would believe – the truth would have many alarmed."

"We cannot pull back – that is not in the plan
So we must get this over and say to each man
That the way to get home is to push extra hard
And not yield to the enemy one single yard."

There was grudging esteem for the spirit and will
Of the Boer who, outnumbered, continued to spill
British blood - and the death-toll continued to mount.
In time, though, the Empire's numbers would count.

The respect for the Boer born atop Spion Kop
Wouldn't lead to the fighting to slow or to stop.
So the war, as all do, formed a character which
Would leave many quite wretched but make a few rich.

But Victoria's death held such matters at bay -
They would be better dealt with on some later day.
With the throne standing vacant, Victoria dead,
The King must take the helm to steer Britain ahead.

The machinery of State was uncovered and primed
Even as the church bells 'round the country had chimed
Out their sorrowful dirges – Britain surely must
Go on just as before with no time to adjust.

Victoria's reign was the greatest, by far,
In the history of Britain - and so popular.
She was born to the throne – it was her obligation
To rise to the moment as head of the nation.

And so it would be for her son and her heir,
Albert Edward, the hope of the people and their
Way of life, their prosperity, the peace they desired -
He had to ascend to the throne as required.

He had been Prince of Wales for so long that he
May have thought his ascension would not come to be
Till the time when he had neither will nor the strength
To take on all his duties – but it came at length.

His cousins, the monarchs of Europe, he knew;
But he also knew that all his options were few.
His mother had thought, as her reign testifies,
She could stop future wars through her family ties.

But she had lived long and her world was restricted
And, by her advisors, politely depicted
As one which would bow to her whim and caprice
And would take, by her Navy, not much to police.

But her son was more worldly – he did know his place
In the order of things – he knew that he must face,
In the future, a war, unless it could be stopped,
In which Europe's young men were disastrously cropped.

The King knew his history, how royalty thought,
How the old days of glory were still being sought.
And he also knew that, quite in spite of their mother,
A spirited prince often murdered his brother.

Great armies were just lethal pawns of a State
No matter how colourful, quaint or ornate
They appeared stepping high in their ranks in a street -
Deployed, they were deadly, not something to greet.

They were there to impose some omnipotent will,
To contest, for a whim, how much blood each would spill.
They were there, someone said, just to do or to die
And quite likely do both - chivalry was a lie.

The King had little power to call or command
Even though he was first in the whole of the land.
His troops may have cheered him when out on parade
But for him to give orders would be a charade.

Although earlier monarchs may well have resented
Arrangements, the King, by this time, represented
The Nation, the State, but the people at large
Looked to Parliament when seeking someone in charge.

As King Edward the Seventh, the Prince must know that
He would be at his best as the prime diplomat
Of his country, his people – but could he succeed
In a world now beset by real fear and such greed?

Would Parliament trust him with matters of State?
Did he understand fully he might complicate
A succession of summits and split an alliance
By wading on in showing regal defiance?

These were matters the Public would never be told
For the workings of State called for temperaments cold
And discussions until ample progress was made -
One false step by the King, one great step retrograde.

So, the King, it would seem, was reduced to a pawn
To be moved into place and then quickly withdrawn;
To be shown to the Public, perhaps unamused -
His power was great but it couldn't be used.

The sad day proceeded, telegrams came and went
From the Palace and Whitehall with news to prevent
Any misunderstanding of what to expect,
What procedures to follow, what words were correct.

Mycroft Holmes was on duty, his presence desired,
For he was one of few who knew what was required
When transition to King by a personage regal
Was made, and what protocols made it all legal.

Every Colony, distant, also each Dominion,
Each power in Europe and each lowly minion
Must hear the sad news and then be reassured
The new King had ascended – the Throne was secured.

It was vital these matters were promptly dealt with.
It was vital for Britain, its kin and its kith,
To know power continued, the nation still served
And was not, by events, one iota unnerved.

At the Palace, that day, the new King would appear
To show he had ascended, to make it quite clear
That all things would proceed as they had done before -
Though Regina was gone, Rex would rule on, he swore.

If turmoil would prevail, Mycroft knew very well
That it might be the time for some courage to swell
In the hearts of opponents who might choose to strike -
He would watch Britain's allies and rivals, alike.

All his agents were out, his assistants recalled -
He would sleep in his office and would be appalled
If a message evaded his ears, even one -
His network, as always, was second-to-none.

Flags were all being lowered, the whole world across,
In respect for the nation which suffered the loss
Of a Queen as the news reached the farthest domain
Of the Earth and the telegraph sang its refrain.

Even those who opposed her were forced to allow
That she was the key link for the time that was 'now'
And the time that was 'then' – most subjects had known
Only VR - the symbol Great Britain had shown.

Any word from her lips meant *"Britannia has spoken."*
While her heir was an unknown, perhaps just a token
Brought out for display and then duly returned,
His demands to wield power, effectively spurned.

However, such notions could turn out quite wrong
And the Prince may have managed to, during his long
And protracted apprenticeship, master the reins
And return Royal Blue to the blood in his veins.

And though stripped of much power, the ascending King
Would resist being dangled aloft on a string
To be lowered on stage when the curtain was raised
To be cheered and paraded and foolishly praised.

He'd refuse to have puppeteers making him move
And have words coming from him he did not approve.
He did know his lines and he would play the game
But would not be a King who ruled only in name.

THE SURVIVORS

McIntyre and Murphy survived and escaped
From the Grimsby debacle and both of them scraped
By for days, daring only to travel by night,
Each one quite unaware of the other one's plight.

Each one had hidden funds to help him disappear;
Not a fortune, as such, but enough to stay clear
Of the clutches of those who would see the two hanged
Or at least have a heavy iron door on them clanged.

They had only to get back to London where cash
Had been hidden away, each man having a stash
Kept at several locations, safe-houses each man
Knew were kept for the comrades-in-arms of Moran.

All the rest had been sacrificed, all left to fend
For themselves, while their target, their Gold dividend,
So they thought, was recaptured and sent on its way.
It had been, they both knew, a disastrous day.

They did not know if war would break out as Moran
Said it would, but it seemed that a sensible man
On the run would leave Britain as fast as he could -
With the Army involved, each man knew that he should.

They expected soldiers would be guarding the stations
And ports with the prospect of war between nations
So high, but discovered that nothing had changed.
What became of the war which Moran had arranged?

They both came to realise the great plan had failed
Probably long before, the Atlantic, they sailed.
Murphy chose to depart with his prospects diminished,
McIntyre would stay, he had business, unfinished.

Percy the Ponce had been caught with the rest
And was finding it difficult not to divest
Himself of every detail which he could recall -
He knew if he didn't, he would take the fall.

He said to Lestrade that, for days, he'd not seen
The 'Big Boss' called Moran or the two who had been
His main agents who were, to him, not known by name
Save for Smith and for Jones nor, what of them, became.

"Mr Smith, an American, was quite reserved,
While the other, called Jones, left a fellow unnerved
By his manner of speaking – Australian, I'd guess -
Each one had found his accent quite hard to suppress."

"Jones went with Moran off to some foreign port -
I wasn't told where - my life would have been short
If I had asked the question. They just went away
Although Jones had returned quite alone yesterday."

"Smith gave nobody orders; he simply observed
What was done and stood by and occasionally swerved
Out of everyone's way, but wrote down the amount
Of the Gold that we lifted; that is, he kept count."

"He went down to the docks, there to wait for the ship
While Jones waited up with us all, cracking the whip
Even though it was me who gave orders to all -
The men looked at each other, ignoring his call."

"He was getting quite testy, we hand things in hand
But it seems he desired to take on command
Of the whole enterprise although most of the fellows
Could not understand his colonial bellows."

"What happened to Jones or to Smith, I can't say -
They got captured or killed, or they got clear away
And are still on the run - I just really don't know
Though I'd say that they'd know well enough to lay low."

"Is that so?" Lestrade countered, *"You must have a bit*
Of an idea of where they would be heading. So sit
Here and think about prospects of scaffold and noose -
Perhaps we may yet get your tongue wagging loose."

"Johnny Roper's Window, I am told, has a view
Rarely seen by the masses, and only a few
Select people are privileged to see such a sight -
I am told it can give them a terrible fright."

"So, think hard, My Old Bucko – a cell or the rope
Are the choices you have, and I certainly hope
You can help us in finding Moran, Smith and Jones.
Tell us all that you know and you might make old bones."

With such options, poor Percy was ready to spill
All the beans that he had – gaol wasn't a thrill
But the noose would be worse, although all he could say
Was, *"Moran wasn't there and his men got away."*

"I don't know where they are but Moran was to be
At the Grimsby rail yards to help out Smith and me
Keeping things moving smoothly, but he wasn't there.
But Jones was erratic, around everywhere."

"Moran always held things right close to his chest.
He would tell what was needed to know, while the rest
Would be kept a close secret and only one man
Would know all the details – and that was Moran."

"No one else but myself and his two special friends
Knew his name was Moran – no one ever pretends
To be needful of knowing much more than he should
For Moran would despatch them as only he could."

Lestrade questioned his prisoners more, hoping to pry
Off a few little morsels on which to rely.
It was clear Percy hadn't much more he could tell -
He own life he would buy but had little to sell.

Meanwhile, Sherlock, to Mycroft, a message would quote
Which he had been delivered by way of a note
And was signed just with 'M', an initial to haunt
The great mind of the Sleuth in the form of a taunt.

Sherlock thought of Moran and blast which destroyed
The ship coming to get all the Gold, and he toyed
With the notion Moran might have set off the blast
Getting rid of that Master of Mayhem at last.

But that did not make sense – Moran wasn't the sort
To take such a way out. While he might well abort
Such a mission as this, he'd be sure to survive
And, from his foe's death, sweet revenge, would derive.

Seeds of doubts on the matter of Moran's demise
Caused Sherlock to consider that it would be wise
To consult with his brother then call for the Tower
Of London to test if these doubt seeds would flower.

There were two hints of note – one concerning the flight
Of a Minister, westward, somewhere, at first light
With no word of his mission nor of his return,
His manner, off-putting and quite taciturn.

The second was that for which Watson had trawled
Seeking big fish to net in a city which sprawled
Like a giant octopus in which millions resided -
What he caught was intriguing, the Tower decided.

Just when Sherlock had wanted to meet with Mycroft,
The news of the death of the Queen sent aloft
Any prospect of getting some time with his brother -
There was no way to tell when they'd see one another.

The Police were too busy controlling the masses
And traffic was flowing like frozen molasses.
Sherlock could do little, Mycroft hadn't time
To assist his young brother in battling crime.

Several days had passed by and Sherlock was incensed
At his failure to understand all, so with tensed
Mental faculties straining, he went to the Yard
Hoping Percy the Ponce hadn't been hit too hard.

*"I hit Percy quite hard, I will freely admit.
But I only used words, though I wouldn't permit
Him to think he'd escape anything he deserved."*
Said Lestrade, adding, *"That got the blighter unnerved."*

"He is not saying much – he's too frightened to move.
He does not wish to hang and he's tried hard to prove
That he worked for Moran but two men, Jones and Smith
Were the ones that Moran had most often worked with."

"Jones and Smith. Very useful." said Holmes with a grin.
"Perhaps the Police Force should pull them all in?"
"Very funny. We might." Lestrade thought to reply,
"You may question each one till your brain starts to fry."

"It is frying, already," said Holmes, *"so desist*
From this prattle and tell me, did Percy assist
You with all your enquiries in any large manner?
Did these men help Moran or was he the sole planner?"

"I can't tell, but I think Percy's telling no lies.
What he's told us, so far, fits right in and complies
With what others have told us, well, those who can speak
Enough English." insisted Lestrade, feeling weak.

"Sherlock Holmes, I am tired, exhausted, in fact.
There is only so much I expect to extract
From a prisoner, short of a stretch on the rack.
I don't even know if Moran made it back."

Sherlock looked at Lestrade with his mouth open wide
Well aware there was more that the man could provide.
He knew his old friend was exhausted but pressed
Him for all that he had, even though he was stressed.

"Back from where? Tell me all. I need data, My Friend,
If this on-going saga is ever to end.
I had not been aware Moran had been away.
Give me all that you have and you'll get sleep today."

"There be no chance of that with the Queen having died.
You can read my report – I don't think Percy lied
But he doesn't know much." Lestrade said with a yawn.
"He recruited the men but, in fact, was a pawn."

"He must have said something about the two men.
The names Smith and Jones are not helpful, so then
Was there more that he said? Any more that he knew?"
Holmes hopefully asked, *"Any more that you drew?"*

"It's all in the report but I will tell you this,"
Said Lestrade standing up for enhanced emphasis,
"Neither one was a Brit - Percy reckons their tones
Would place Smith from America, elsewhere for Jones."

"This Smith was at Grimsby awaiting Moran
Who had gone off abroad, which was as per the plan,
Taking Jones who returned to help out with the plot -
Moran wasn't with him – in the plan, that was not."

"Percy said he thought Jones had a military past
By the way he gave orders – he seemed to think fast
On his feet and insisted that things be secure -
From Australia, he guessed, though he couldn't be sure."

"From Australia, you say." Holmes repeated, surprised,
"And a military man, so this Percy surmised.
That is very intriguing, My very tired Friend.
Percy may be reprieved from the noose in the end."

"Well, this is something new, it's really quite thrilling.
I think Percy must undergo some more grilling,
This time to be asked of somebody called Mack -
McIntyre, that is – it is time to attack."

"Get the blighter awake and up here." Lestrade growled
To a Constable while, toward Sherlock, he scowled
Knowing well he had open a great hornet's nest -
He had no hope whatever of getting some rest.

A few minutes passed and Holmes told what he knew
To Lestrade while he asked if some more of the crew
Might be eager for mercy. Could he tell them to give
Up the names of those men if they wanted to live?

"We have little on them, less than we would wish
And, it seems, few among them speak any English
Though they understand much when I mention a rope.
There are too many of them for us here to cope."

"They all seem to be claiming they simply signed on
For a bit of hard work to the north of London
And were waiting for someone to give them the call
When the Army charged in and arrested them all."

"They are foreigners, all; some have papers to show
And are all acting innocent, so I don't know
If there's much we can prove – I'd get rid of the lot -
I don't think they knew much of the overall plot."

"But, here's Percy – perhaps he'll be able to give
You the name that you're seeking. He does want to live
And we've got him for robbery, not murder, as yet
But we'll get some more on him – on that you can bet."

Percy looked like a schoolboy about to be whipped
By a scowling headmaster – he silently slipped
To his chair as directed and slumped like a cur -
He had no indication of what might occur.

Lestrade shouted at Percy, *"Sit straight, will you, Man.*
You can help yourself now, otherwise you just can
Go back down to your cell till you rot or you hang
Like the rest of the scum in your miserable gang."

"Listen, Percy, the man at my side's on a task
And has got a few questions he's eager to ask.
If you answer correctly, there is a faint hope
That you won't end your life at the end of a rope."

"His name's Sherlock Holmes; he's the famous detective
Who you will have heard of – he's very effective
At finding out things no one else ever can
So, if you want to live, don't play games with this man."

"If there's something you know, I advise you speak up
And don't grovel about like some mangy young pup.
Mr Holmes has come here in a great deal of haste
And, on someone like you, has no time he can waste."

Sherlock looked at the prisoner, cringing and cowered
Now that he had nothing to make him empowered,
Not one single thug who could back-up a threat -
All the fellow could do was just sit there and sweat.

In his typical manner, quite gentle but firm,
Sherlock spoke to the prisoner, who'd started to squirm,
Hoping he could remember the real name of Jones,
"Now, the Law confers mercy on he who atones."

"You have not led a life which one might declare good
And they've caught you red-handed, that is understood.
You are not unintelligent – that, we both know,
Nor am I – so, with answers, do not be too slow."

"I will ask of a fellow who had you employed
In a plot to steal Gold, that someone who'd deployed
His resources to divert a train and then take
Off its cargo, a cargo I'll tell you was fake."

"Fake." uttered Percy, *"Just what are you saying?*
What sort of a game with me are you now playing?
I saw and I felt all those boxes of Gold -
Each box far too heavy for one man to hold"

Sherlock looked right at Percy and gave him a smile
Which he held, keeping Percy confused for a while.
Leaning forward, he rolled both his eyes and replied,
"My Friend, in those boxes, no Gold had you spied."

"I can tell you right here, what was stolen was Lead.
It was covered with Gold paint a long time ahead
Of the move we expected – we wanted the man
Who had put into action this darstardly plan."

"We know of Moran; we don't know where he is
And we know the original plan wasn't his
But belonged to another, a man now long dead
But whose plan Moran thought to deploy in his stead."

"So, tell me of Moran. When did you see him last?
And when you have told me of him, you may cast
Your mind back to those two, his lieutenants perhaps.
What can you tell me of those mystery chaps?"

"Think hard. Opportunity's knocking, My Friend.
If you answer correctly, your days you may end
In a prison, for sure, although not the Old Dart -
You'll give me the answers I need, if you're smart."

"Mr Holmes, I have told the Police all I know.
I worked for Moran but have nothing to show.
You've caught what turned out a quite miserable gang."
Said Percy, distraught, hoping he wouldn't hang.

"If there's more I can tell, I don't know what it is
For the plan was Moran's and those men were both his,
Not recruited by me – and Moran didn't share
Information with underlings, you'd be aware."

"Moran isn't the sort to confide in his men
Till the time's right to know, one must wait until then
And not ask any questions he doesn't want asked."
Sherlock pushed him, however, to get them unmasked.

"That is true, I concede, but perhaps one had let
Down his guard for a moment – I have never met
Anyone who, when busy, would not give away
Hints to what he was thinking – to let his thoughts stray."

"Well, now that you ask me, I think I recall
That I once overheard those two men of his call
Moran something like 'madman' in anger, then one
Had said straight to the other 'he'll bring us undone'."

"That was just before Jones and Moran went away,
To arrange for the ship for the Gold, I would say.
Moran said they'd return to make sure all went well
But Jones came back alone, as far as I could tell."

"Moran wasn't there at the railway yards
And I'd say, if I guessed, it would be on the cards
That Moran had been murdered by Jones on that boat.
I don't know how to prove it – perhaps he will float."

"Perhaps will not do it." Sherlock Holmes then retorted,
  "You must know more worthy of being reported."
Percy, almost shouting, to Sherlock came back:
"Yes, now I remember – Moran called Jones 'Mack'."

THE FUNERAL

At Victoria's death, Albert Edward ascended
The throne of Great Britain – an era had ended.
He would not be crowned till the following year
But, that things would be different, was perfectly clear.

Thus, the old House of Hanover came to an end -
Four Georges, one William, before it could send,
To the throne, a Victoria, Empress and Queen -
The dynasty, almost two centuries, had seen.

Victoria's late consort, Prince Albert, conferred
On his son, the new Monarch of Britain, referred
To as Edward the Seventh, a new regal name -
Saxe-Coburg and Gotha his new House became.

A new name would appear on new forms to be printed,
A new face stamped upon every coin that was minted -
A new century, and a new understanding
Of power and people and who was commanding.

The old notions were fading and could not resist
A great wave of reform which swept in to insist
That the powers of old be relinquished and given
To those down below who, to govern, had striven.

Calls had come for the Crown to be banished forever
And the heirs of its bearer to carry it, never.
The old order should just, some insisted, dissolve -
Some, to force revolution, declared their resolve.

To many, Victoria stood as the 'Mother
Of Britain' - they could not conceive of another
Who would cruel the peace that Britannia had wrought -
They wanted no other, no other was sought.

But her son, in his prime, had brought many to tears
With his playboy existence - so many had fears
Of those noted excesses he seemed not to quell.
The 'Father of Britain' did not fit him well.

Voltaire once had said that the government best
That a nation could ever, on itself, invest
Was a Monarch quite wise but restricted by Law -
Constitutional Monarchy, what he foresaw.

While in exile in Britain, its freedoms he noted,
And as all of his writings persistently quoted,
Were expressed in the Law and respected by Kings
Though the people had ways to clip errant royal wings.

Edward knew of the mood of the people far more
Than his critics had ever admitted before.
He also knew power and how it was used -
He knew it was real and it could be abused.

But before anything could be brought into play,
Victoria would, in a time-honoured way,
Be farewelled in a funeral befitting her reign -
The grief most would feel, nobody would feign.

All the crowned heads of Europe would surely attend
Which, to all revolutionaries, would recommend
A quite opportune target for bullet or bomb
That is, if assassins maintained great aplomb.

Security would be, of course, well enhanced
And it would be a desperate person who chanced
Getting close – anyone of suspicion would find
He was in for a grilling of unpleasant kind.

It was at Osborne House on the Isle of Wight
That Victoria sank, at the onset of night,
Into peace and to history, taking her leave
Of a world which would all, of her passing, bereave.

The Alberta would sail her to Portsmouth to be
Carried onto Victoria Station where she
Would be taken through London to Paddington and
Then be carried to Windsor – her wish and command.

Her funeral cortège to the Castle would pass
Through the town where her people of every class
Would be lining the streets as her carriage passed by,
Though some panic ensued as something went awry.

The scene at the station had turned somewhat manic -
The gun-carriage horses were subject to panic
When something had caused them to jostle and trip
And the harness which held them to give way and rip.

But quick thinking by sailors got things settled down -
They replaced the harness and, right through the town
And without any horses, a path they would forge
As they pulled the gun-carriage right on to St George.

In that Chapel, her funeral, attended by those
Of her family and special attendees they chose,
Would be held, after which, the Queen, lying-in-state
For two days, would lie next to her dear Albert, late.

At the Castle, Victoria's descendents discussed
Matters which might have left her upset and nonplussed
For, although blood relations, those present debated
The Empire's power which one, at least, hated.

King Edward, also, had an intense dislike
Of his nephew, the Kaiser Wilhelm, who might strike
When he could to expand across Europe's extent -
He was confused, yet fearful, of Wilhelm's intent.

But when news of a possible threat on the King
Came to light, all agreed that the obvious thing
Not to do was show fear and to cower behind
Castle walls – they united and clung to their kind.

But the mood in the Castle was sombre, as well,
And was mournful as far as those outside could tell.
Respect had to be paid and things couldn't be rushed
And the talks, while intense, must appear to be hushed.

With her two days of lying-in-state at an end,
Victoria's cortège formed, waiting to send
Upon her final journey, the Empress of old -
Princes and Princesses said prayers in the cold.

With formalities finished, as had been prescribed,
The cortège then proceeded in weather described
As appallingly frigid, trees barren and bare,
And the Monarch, of lingering danger, aware.

Into Windsor Great Park, the group slowly made way
To the Royal Mausoleum, there gently to lay,
To her rest, the great lady, the Empress and Queen,
The likes of which no other nation had seen.

After mourners returned to the Castle, a sigh
Of relief was released, for the risk had been high
That a dogged assassin was trying to kill
The new King – an assassin with murderous skill.

The King had been surrounded by soldiers in ranks -
He was guarded in front and behind and on flanks
But, to shield him from dangers of every sort
Was a task, nigh impossible, aides would report.

Between death and interment, a full thirteen days
Had elapsed, stalling efforts in so many ways
For the author of Sherlock Holmes' note to be found -
This mysterious 'M' could have long gone to ground.

Holmes wasn't put off by the difficulties posed.
He had Watson to help him - he'd anxiously nosed
His way all around London; he plagued Scotland yard
For the access he needed, though going was hard.

Police leave had been cancelled - all were on alert
And, from high, received orders they should not divert
Any time other than which was urgently sought -
If it wasn't a murder then, drop it, they ought.

But, of course, Lestrade knew of Moran and his plot
To rob banks of their Gold, but he felt he had got
Almost all of the felons involved on the day
And had no time to chase those who got clean away.

But he also knew Watson who said that he should
Hear out Sherlock's concerns and give help if he could.
Daniel Jakes of the Tower suggested he ought,
For suspicions most dire, to light, had been brought.

Sherlock's brother, Mycroft, had been up to his ears
Helping out with procedures and calming the fears
Of a Government seemingly always on edge
Sitting, over a precipice, right on its ledge.

Dan told Sherlock to push Percy right to the brink -
Show the fellow his options and then let him think
That he'd wear the hemp collar if he didn't give
What was needed. Did he wish to die or to live?

But when Percy said 'Mack', Sherlock knew he must act
And not let the objections of Mycroft detract
From his need to be told of this man on the run
Who was probably vengeful, and good with a gun.

Holmes knew that he had been a soldier of note
Bringing battle to Boers in a region remote.
But now he was here with an attitude bad
In the pay of Moran – to know why, he'd be glad.

"Could that fellow be 'M' and, if so, might he try
To cause trouble in London but, if so, then why
Would he taunt me with notes of a quite cryptic sort?
I have a bad feeling, but naught to report."

"Was Moran really dead?" Sherlock asked of himself.
"Can I put the closed folder of his on my shelf
And rejoice in the loss of a dangerous man?
I would if I could but I don't think I can."

Of that other man, Smith, there was no way to know
If he'd join up with Jones, that is Mack, and then throw
Into chaos, together, the changeover, royal.
Would these two, to each other, stay faithful and loyal?

Of the little he knew of this Smith, Sherlock might
Make a judgement that he'd, out of Britain, take flight.
But, if things told of Jones had, of truth, just a scrap,
He was bound to present a most dangerous chap.

Sherlock made the decision to force Mycroft's hand
By invading his office where he would demand
That he'd listen, at least, to what he had to say -
He would tell him an outrage might well be in play.

Mycroft, now convinced he at least ought to meet
With his brother, said, *"Just wait for me in the street
In a Hansom – I'll come out and we'll drive away
And discuss what we need to – it's vital, I pray."*

*"I will bring a four-wheeler, we've Watson and Jakes
Who will come along with us – they have what it takes,
As we saw once before, just a short while ago."*
Sherlock said, adding further, *"So do not say 'No'."*

The two brothers descended and met the two men
Down below in the street to discuss what and when
There just might be a threat of a devilish kind
Which may well be a figment of Sherlock's great mind.

*"Something is afoot, I am certain of that,
For the trap which we sprung missed a rather large rat
Who has travelled to London, as likely as not."*
Declared Holmes, *"Though suspicion is all I have got."*

Trotting slowly 'round London, in secret they spoke
Each explaining to Mycroft why he might invoke
More security for the Queen's funeral processions
All from hints gathered from just an odd few confessions.

McIntyre, in the meantime, had made his way back
Into London deciding to get on the track
Of the King who he chose as his target to strike,
The King of a nation he'd come to dislike.

At a safe house Moran had long kept under lock,
Mack, the would-be assassin, could hide and restock
With provisions and cash and rearm with a gun
Which Moran once described as the ultimate fun.

He could watch as the nation displayed its dismay
At Victoria's passing – attention he'd pay
To the details of funeral arrangements advised -
His vengeance would be the best he had devised.

In London, there'd be little chance of success
With provisions for safety, he had to confess.
So, around Windsor Station, he'd do it instead -
Before reaching the Castle, the King would be dead.

He knew just how difficult that it would be -
A challenge most complex for which only he
Had the ultimate weapon - silence was assured -
A replacement air-gun which Moran had procured.

He might well hit the King – he had reason to think
That, if he concentrated and didn't once blink,
He had quite a good chance for a lone deadly shot -
Vengeance would be his for Moran's failed plot.

At ground level, he said, *"Not a bat's chance in Hell*
That I'd get close to Edward, he's guarded too well."
But up high at an angle he felt he could fire
At least once at the man of his fury's desire.

He selected a site near the station where he
Could take aim at the Monarch, a site which would be
Close to where the royal cortège would assemble -
For success, he'd need nerve – his hand mustn't tremble.

On the roof he'd be seen, quite as likely as not,
So a top-storey window would serve as a spot
To take aim at the King – he'd move in well before
The cortège was expected – he couldn't do more.

But the angle presented was very oblique,
A difficult shot but a rather unique
Opportunity to kill the new King and escape
While the crowd milled around only able to gape.

He knew well he'd be in for a nation's abuse
Though he'd never use this as a feeble excuse
Not to carry his plan to its ultimate end -
He did not have a conscience with which to contend.

As the Naval contingent marched solemnly by,
McIntyre, gun loaded and primed, had to try
To keep still, absolutely - the gun-carriage trailed
Behind horses, all white, as the Queen had detailed.

A gun-carriage would carry her coffin as she
Had expressly directed – it was meant to be
A symbolic expression of military strength,
Perhaps a last word to be given at length.

But the horses weren't used to such bustle and noise
And, as Mack squeezed the trigger, one lost all its poise
Jumping sideways obstructing the bullet's objective -
Mack's attempt on the King had been quite ineffective.

Though the King wasn't injured, the bullet collided
With force on a buckle through which had been guided
A harness connecting the gun-carriage to
The white horses which had behaved well, hitherto.

The white horses reared up, but attendants caught all
Before panic set in, then someone thought to call
On the sailors ahead to rig harnesses, new,
And they pulled the gun-carriage, the entire crew.

McIntyre thought no one suspected a thing -
The man, though incensed over missing the King,
Had to make his escape through the melée below -
For his efforts, again, he had nothing to show.

He had one opportunity left when the King
Would be vulnerable – he might risk everything
On a final attempt to avenge what he saw
As betrayal when he had been forced to withdraw.

THE SUSPICION

As the story went 'round that the sailors had saved
The Queen's dignity, all who had heard it had raved
At the presence of mind which was shown at the time
Unaware that, in play, was an unfinished crime.

Sherlock Holmes read the story and, too, was impressed
But was also suspicious so, quickly, he dressed
And proceeded to Whitehall, to Mycroft once more -
He must see that harness – he'd questions galore.

Before any Royal mourners had gathered to lay
The Grandmother of Europe to rest and to pay
Last respects to the Empress and Queen, Sherlock met
With his brother to tell him of more danger, yet.

He had no actual proof, but his nose for a crime
Told him something was brewing and in a short time
An event would occur to send Britain askew -
That event would be violent, that much Sherlock knew.

He suspected a threat, now he knew this was fact
But to get a response he'd need data exact.
From his brother he'd seek the assistance he'd need -
To his office he'd, without any notice, proceed.

"Mycroft, hear me out," Sherlock said, storming in
To the office of Mycroft, his head in a spin
With excitement that he found quite hard to contain.
"Forgive me, Dear brother, but let me explain."

"That a horse might rear up, I would have to accept,
But the Royal Horse Artillery ought to expect
That a horse might well do so and keep it restrained
By experienced handlers who'd have things contained."

"It would seem the white horses were chosen by She,
Our late Empress, who said such a Queen ought to be
Carried on a gun-carriage pulled slowly along
By white horses, not black - that is if I'm not wrong."

134

"That is so," replied Mycroft, *"we honoured that wish*
Even though those white horses were somewhat skittish
Being new to the harness and unused to noise -
In such circumstances, even I could lose poise."

Sherlock gave a wry smile then continued to say,
"There might be nothing in this or something in play
Which we must not ignore – I need help to proceed.
I have questions to ask and it's answers I need."

"An artillery horse is conditioned to pull
Heavy loads over uneven ground at a full
Reckless gallop with shouting and canons afire -
A horse which would panic, one would not desire."

"One needs strength, also stamina, in such a horse
For to have it break down would lead on to remorse
In the midst of a battle – likewise every strap
Has to hold under tension and must never snap."

"But a harness did snap when it ought to have not
For the strain put upon it was modest – a trot
Would have been most unseemly, the going was slow
And, so, why it should break I am quite keen to know."

"Well, the horse did rear up." replied Mycroft intrigued
At the thoughts of his brother and, although fatigued
From two weeks of poor sleep and a thousand requests,
Said, *"But Brother, find out what this detail suggests."*

"I will do so if given a hand that is free."
Replied Sherlock, *"However, I'll need some degree*
Of authority if I am ever to speak
To the Army, otherwise my prospects will be bleak."

135

"It's a world to itself, full of military bluster;
A realm of intrigue rarely able to muster
A sense of cooperative public existence -
Frustration will be the reward for persistence."

"But give it a war and it jumps into action;
Likewise, direct orders get some satisfaction
For I'll get direct answers to questions I ask
But to hope for much more is a frustrating task."

"Well, that war is upon us - our enemy's here
On our very own streets and it will persevere
Till an outrage is done upon Edward, our King.
Or the Kaiser, perhaps? What a war that would bring."

"I must locate that harness so I may inspect
It for signs of a weakness or, as I suspect,
For the signs that, a bullet, its buckle had struck -
That the horses were flighty that day was good luck."

"Good luck for the King and the Country, I'd say,"
Mycroft spluttered, *"that is, if it happened that way.*
I have great respect for your sensitive nose,
So let's see what more sniffing can further expose."

"I will need to determine," Sherlock curtly stated,
"The fate of that harness. It must be located
For, if there was damage by bullet to see,
The King's life is in danger, you must then agree."

"No gunshot was heard – well, none that was reported."
Sherlock said to his brother through features contorted
By fear and dismay at what this had implied -
"The thought of an air-gun leaves me terrified."

"An air-gun was favoured and used by Moran
To kill Ronald Adair. Either he or the man
Known as Mack could be using a similar gun.
Being silent and deadly, that thought I would shun."

"But shun it, I shan't, nor dare I ever shrink
From the notion that we might be brought to the brink
Of a war by one bullet - perhaps revolution -
My Brother, for this, we must find the solution."

"I have left word for Watson - a brave man, you know -
To again meet us here with a carriage below
In the street. That is if, any time, you may spare.
I myself, to presume to insist, wouldn't dare."

"With luck, Jakes will be with him – he knows his way
Around people and won't let them lead us astray
By evading our questions or giving false leads -
He's a man who, the most subtle character, reads."

"To St. John's Wood Barracks," said Mycroft, *"We'll go*
And we'll look at that harness to tell if or no
That a bullet had rendered its buckle unfit
To hold harness together or if it just split."

As Mycroft left his office, a bag was received
Full of recent despatches, though he had perceived
It essential the group should now get underway -
He wanted to hear what the rest had to say.

He would take the bag with him, a thing rarely done,
But he needed to know if there could be someone
Who attempted to kill either Kaiser or King.
On the way he'd have time to peruse everything.

To the carriage he jumped with Sherlock right behind
And called out to the driver, *"Now never you mind
About comfort or danger – off to St John's Wood,
To the barracks at high speed. Is that understood?"*

The driver said nothing but cracked a loud whip
Over two rested horses which started to clip
A fast trot on the cobbles, though Watson enquired,
"Aren't those barracks in Whitehall the ones we desired?"

"No!" replied Mycroft, *"They're mostly for show.
But they can be quite deadly and could strike a blow
If the need for protection arises, My friend.
They would not have the harness, I'm bound to contend."*

*"We'll not find it in Whitehall so we must proceed
With all haste to those barracks where we should indeed
Find that harness held over for later inquest -
We don't want it discarded, so let us not rest."*

The group advanced northward and took a turn west,
The group spoke together, intending to test
Every notion of Sherlock's, each logical guess,
Although, to despatches, Mycroft would digress.

*"It is paramount I keep on top of my mail.
I attend to it promptly and will never fail
To take note of its content, no matter how strange.
There are so many matters I have to arrange."*

Mycroft opened each envelope making his mark
On its face and its contents while keeping a stark
And unmoveable countenance, noting each fact
For significance and for its meaning, exact.

He had read through a dozen despatches or more
When he startled his comrades as never before
With a cry of, *"Eureka! This is a good turn -
Get the horses whipped up, we have miles to burn."*

*"It says here, from the Navy, three bodies were found
Washed ashore close together with one of them bound
In a sack, stabbed to death in the chest they suggest,
While the other two drowned, says an early inquest."*

*"They had all washed ashore upon Bridlington Bay
To the north of the Humber. Not so far away
From your Grimsby Docks' battle, I hasten to say.
They were three who quite clearly did not get away."*

*"One drowned man is unknown, just a sailor it states,
While the second had papers suggesting he rates
As a mercantile Captain called Meyer who hailed
From the Netherlands from which he'd recently sailed."*

*"But the man in a bag had tattoos which suggested
The Indian Army, so they had suggested
A search through the records to seek out this man -
He fits the description of Colonel Moran!"*

"One less rat to be trapped." declared Sherlock with glee.
*"The whole world is made better now that it is free
Of one more of the vermin I swore to remove
From the face of the earth – of this news, I approve."*

*"But it also points to my conjecture being sound -
That at least one more felon is yet to be found.
McIntyre we must seek, this Mack we must find,
It must not come to pass, what this man has in mind."*

In their quest for the harness, the group had to trace
A long trail through a city in mourning at pace
With no thought to slow down - of the essence, was time,
If they were to prevent a despicable crime.

Northward they had travelled, then turned to the west
Along Marylebone Road, into Baker to rest
While Holmes made a dash to the door, at great speed,
Of Two-Twenty-One-B to select what he'd need.

A microscope, certainly, so he might show
Any tell-tale marks of a bullet-like blow
To the men who must guard both the cortège and King
And convince them to strengthen their protective ring.

And perhaps, a reagent responding to Lead,
Which might prove that a bullet was fired instead
Of the harness just breaking – Mycroft might insist
That, requests to postpone, they ought not to resist.

Then onward north-westerly right along Park
Onto Wellington Road, then to Barracks where stark
Faces told of a military guard on patrol -
It was clear, from here on, who would be in control.

But Mycroft had a document, magic, it seemed,
And the soldiers who saw it instinctively deemed
Him to be a superior personage to
Be promptly obeyed – what he said, they would do.

The Deputy Commandant came at the run
But, before any search by the group had begun,
Mycroft had been informed that the harness he sought
Wasn't there and, to search Windsor Castle, he ought.

He returned to his colleagues, chagrin on his face,
Saying despondently, *"We are at the wrong place.*
These are the home barracks of those whom we seek
But they've been gone from here for well over a week."

"That contingent's at Windsor, so I have been told.
It is too far for travel and also too cold
To have horses and men moving more than required."
Said Mycroft, *"It's there, that harness we desired."*

"I've arranged for our horses to be substituted
For two stabled here – they are quite undisputed
As prime types with stamina, courage and pluck
And will get us to Windsor in good time, with luck."

"We must be off now – on to Windsor we start.
When our horses are changed it is time to depart
But there's food to be had in the mess, I am told -
There's no need of us being both hungry and cold."

"So eat what you can – in some bags we may carry
Away what we'll need – there is no time to tarry.
Windsor's been informed to expect our arrival.
They've been told that the matter is one of survival."

The hours went by but the horses kept on
At a good steady pace to that great bastion,
Windsor Castle, where absolute proof that a shot
Had been fired at someone they'd find or would not.

Detained for some time at the huge castle gate,
The four men on a mission were locked in debate
With a guard who had orders to keep out or shoot
Anyone who forced entry - then talk would be moot.

Mycroft came to the fore with his document, magic,
Demanding to enter with warnings of tragic
Events to transpire if he wasn't let in -
Jakes wanted to hit the man right on the chin.

As the scene overheated, an officer called
To the guards at the gate, by this time somewhat galled,
They should let them all in and explained, mortified,
"The guards have had orders to shoot if defied."

"The Guard had been changed a few minutes before
You arrived. I apologise and I deplore
The delay you experienced – the guards did the task
To which they were assigned – no less of them I'd ask."

"They had not been advised of your visit, I fear,
For the previous Guard had been told, loud and clear,
To expect several men of quite eminent standing
Who, to enter the Castle, would soon be demanding."

"We had not given names – we preferred to keep mute
On the need for your visit which might constitute
A most ominous portent of imminent strife -
The rumours, of course, would be sure to be rife."

"Well, we're here and there's critical work we must do
So we won't dwell on why or, for that matter, who
Might be shot by the guards over querulous trifles."
Said Mycroft, *"Our visit involves other rifles."*

Major Wilkes uttered, *"Rifles? The message declared*
You required the gun-carriage harness which fared
Rather poorly by breaking – of guns, I don't know
So a reason to stay here you now ought to show."

"I have heard of the harness you're after - the one
Which broke and almost brought the cortège undone.
For that item, we've searched high and low everywhere;
We've quizzed anyone we could find who was there."

Mycroft showed him the document stating that he
Had the highest authority needed to be
Offered entry and all the assistance required,
Though the reticence shown by the guards, he admired.

"On the subject of rifles, my brother desires
To examine the harness – he often enquires
About rifles and trifles like bullet impacts
Upon buckles – the man deals in obscure facts."

The Major looked worried – he hadn't been told
About bullet impacts – he'd been left in the cold
Of the reason that this quite official foursome,
To Windsor, just to look at some harness, had come.

But he told what he knew which was not good to hear
By Mycroft and his colleagues who started to fear
They would never have time to confirm what they felt
To be fact – for that harness would make a good belt.

"Well, the harness was cut from the gun-carriage and
Was discarded, I'm told, and picked up by a band
Of what all the sailors called souvenir hunters.
You might check the Pubs and enquire of their punters."

"They might cut it in sections and sell the thing off
And, before anyone of you chances to scoff,
I will tell you they'll sell it for all they can get
Which might be in the hundreds of pounds, I would bet."

"I suggest, go to town and search all of the Pubs
But be wary of getting the fiercest of snubs
Should you sound like Authority coming down hard -
Their bouncers are worse than the worst Castle guard."

"If you do find a bullet mark, what does this bode?
The King and the Kaiser are bound to explode
If another security measure is placed
On the funeral arrangements – their ire I've faced."

"They are bound to refuse to be hidden away
Within some armoured wagon – I know they will say
To 'bring on any danger – we shall not be cowed
And no changes for safety's sake shall be allowed'."

"So, whatever you find, they will not be deterred
From parading around – I should know, I've conferred
With their aides about keeping a sensible border.
I trust what I'm saying is not out of order."

"I judge I can freely express what I feel.
Your talk about bullets tells me we should steel
Ourselves for a strike on the life of the King
Or the Kaiser, so I will discuss anything."

"Their two minds are quite rigidly focussed on pride.
Between Britain and Germany is a divide
Which just getting wider, I'm forced to admit,
And refusals to budge don't surprise me one bit."

"A friendly contest between cousins is bunk.
The Kaiser, it seems, wants a much greater chunk
Of the world and is jealous of Britain's dominions
Even though each refutes all such harmful opinions."

144

"Seek your harness, by all means, but hear what I say -
Neither bullet nor bomb will cause either to stray
From the course now decided – it's much like a race
And the first to seek shelter is bound to lose face."

THE PUBS

Sherlock said to his brother, *"I fear this is true*
And that, even if we find a definite clue,
Those two men will ignore any danger ahead
Till the bullets are fired and they're both lying dead."

"Still, we must try to find out if any attempt
Had been made to shoot either or both, for contempt
Each might show for his safety endangers us all
And, despite their objections, great care is the call."

"We should make out a Pub list, including locations,
And proceed with short questions, not interrogations,
And explaining it's urgent the buckle be found -
Just say all royal harnesses might be unsound."

"Say it's vital we find it and say a reward
Will be offered to those who would lead us toward
The location of that most particular buckle
But be careful of fakes and the odd wayward knuckle."

"For we're off to a world where suspicion is rife
And recourse to the fists is an old way of life
Which inhabitants feel marks each one as a man
So they challenge outsiders each chance that they can."

"Watson, come with me, we're a definite team.
Mycroft, you and Jakes should be building up steam
For a journey which Jakes will have been on before
And might well inform Mycroft of what is in store."

"Major Wilkes might supply us with just such a list
With the help of his soldiers who, I might insist,
Would know every bar within ten mile's range.
If they didn't, I'd suggest all his men had gone strange."

"Mycroft, we are off to a world full of vice,
Not to mention the fleas and the huge plagues of lice.
But we fear there's a plot which is ready to hatch
So, for your King and Country, get ready to scratch."

"I'm scratching already." Mycroft said in reply,
"But I'm certainly ready to give it a try.
For a harness and buckle, I'll go in pursuit
But if I had been warned, I'd have worn an old suit."

Again they changed horses - the driver complained,
But was rather excited when Sherlock explained
That he would be rewarded for all he had done -
His efforts, so far, had been second-to-none.

At St John's Wood barracks, his original team
Of matched horses were stabled along with the cream
Of artillery horses – the grooms would take care
Of his four-legged friends, serving best oaten fare.

Seven Pubs had been listed as places to check
Even though, going in, each might stick out his neck
For he might be resented – this world he'd invade
Might not welcome his questions – disputes, he'd evade.

Holmes, Watson and Jakes, such a job, would embrace
But the wild card was Mycroft, a man out of place
When it came to the Public, the greater unwashed
As he often spoke of them – his fears must be quashed.

Jakes would do all the talking, Mycroft would observe
And decide if responses they got would deserve
To be taken as true or rejected as lie.
Could they, such responses, to McIntyre, tie?

Three Pubs they would enter and three times they'd fail
To obtain information – and to no avail
Would Mycroft's insight be invoked on that night.
Perhaps Sherlock and Watson, do better, just might

But Sherlock and Watson had failed as well
And, on McIntyre's movements, had nothing to tell.
No news of the lost broken harness was found.
Information, they'd none – their frustration, profound.

Three Pubs they had entered and came out with nought,
Not the least indication of that which they sought.
The fourth on their list was the one where they'd meet
Up with Mycroft and Jakes – it was just down the street.

First to get there would wait for the others to come
But Mycroft and Jakes had both found it irksome
To be out in the cold on a miserable night
So to wait for the others inside they just might.

As they entered, the drone from the drinkers abated -
The pair was surveyed and felt intimidated.
One looked like a copper, the other presented
The look of a landlord who they all resented.

The Publican spoke up with, *"What will it be?*
You have both lost your way, it's apparent to me."
Mycroft said, *"We'll just wait for our friends to arrive."*
Thinking that, till the morning, they might not survive.

The Publican gave a disparaging look
At the pair as he picked up a bottle and shook
His head slowly – his Pub was a place people came
For a drink and he thought their response a bit lame.

"You might wait for a train but in here we serve drinks
To whoever comes in. So it's lager, methinks,
That you gents might desire, or whiskey, perhaps.
So, what will it be my two over-dressed chaps?"

Before either could speak a large fellow approached
And upon Mycroft's personal space had encroached.
"W-hat is it you w-want?", he said with a stutter -
Mycroft felt that his accent belonged in the gutter.

"Well, nothing from you. Get away, Little Man."
Mycroft said to a fellow of gigantic span
Whom he obviously held in the utmost disdain
And, from making more comment, he could not refrain.

Big Henry had fists which could double for hammers
And did not take to Mycroft who said, *"All your stammers*
Are caused by your need for more motherly care
And quite obviously she had none she could spare."

Well, Big Henry, saw red and he grabbed Mycroft's coat
With his left while his right almost circled his throat.
He lifted his arm and Mycroft nearly strangled
As in front of the patrons he gingerly dangled.

Big Henry dropped Mycroft who took a deep breath
After seeing a vision of imminent death,
But he then took a blow on the tip of his nose -
Mycroft fell, and the dispute had come to a close.

Holmes and Watson had heard the commotion and ran
To the Pub to see what had ensued as a man
Ran out yelling, *"Big Henry's just levelled a toff
And is likely to knock the fool blighter's head off."*

With Mycroft sprawled out on the beer-splattered floor,
His brother, Sherlock, burst in through the main door
To be followed by Watson who held back a grin
While Jakes was declaring he'd run Henry in.

Sherlock shouted, *"Stand back, I've a Doctor in tow
And this man needs his help, so I hope you will show
Just a little regard for a man on his back -
I'll buy drinks for you all if you'll stop this attack."*

He laid down one Fiver and then laid another
While Watson, the Doctor, attended his brother
Who'd started to moan and to mumble and mutter
In a manner which might challenge Big Henry's stutter.

The Publican charged out from behind the bar
And he confronted Jakes who had started to spar
With Big Henry. He threatened to crack any head
Which belonged to those fighting, not drinking instead.

A truce of a sort was immediately called
As the cudgel was waved and the argument stalled.
The Publican gazed at this group with a grin -
Sherlock Holmes, to his Pub, had just wandered in.

"Mr Holmes! Is it you? Well, this is a surprise.
But your friend on the floor, I must say, was unwise
To insult poor Big Henry. He's not very bright
But I think I might say that he knows how to fight."

"Billy Jenkins - remember. I got put away
For a trivial case about jewels gone astray.
They had me for murder but you proved them wrong -
I was set for the drop until you came along."

"Six months, the beak gave me and buried the rope.
I was sweating profusely but you gave me hope
Of a chance to survive when I was to be hanged.
I felt great relief as my cell door was banged."

"So, what brings you here into my humble Pub?
Did your friends lose their way on a trip to the club
Or are you on a case? That's it! Can I be
Of assistance? If so, what you will, ask of me."

Sherlock didn't look up because Mycroft had grunted.
His face was all bloody, his nose had been shunted,
It seemed, from one side of his face to the other.
"This man on your floor is my fool elder brother."

"Can you bring me a towel? It will help stem the flow
Of my brother's life blood – he is starting to show
Signs of resurgent life. Yes Jenkins, it's true,
In your case, I discovered the critical clue."

"I see you have prospered – your life has improved
But I'm looking for something which somebody moved
From where it was discarded right after it broke.
But I am also seeking a desperate bloke."

150

"A desperate bloke? Well they're not really rare
But I might be of help in this case if you'd care
To tell me what he looks like, or give me his name."
Replied Jenkins, *"If I can't, then it would be a shame."*

Sherlock said he might be of some help in this case.
"This man must be flushed out before any chase
Can begin – there is danger, extreme, if we can't.
He's a dangerous man so, to give up, we shan't."

"Can we speak? It's important – in private is best.
I have things I would ask you, and also the rest
Of those here on the premises later, perhaps.
It concerns royal carriages and broken straps."

"I'm confused." Jenkins uttered, *"you said it's a man*
That you're all seeking after, then asked if we can
Speak of carriages, royal, and straps which have broken.
I believe there is much that you have left unspoken."

"You must give me your word that you'll not say a thing.
This concerns, I must tell you, the life of the King
And the peace we enjoy in these islands of ours.
If we fail, then all that we hold sacred sours."

"A harness gave way as the Queen's coffin travelled
Through town and events would soon have unravelled
If not for the actions of sailors who made
Quick repairs – it was lucky they were on parade."

"That harness was discarded but I need to see
If the thing had just broken or if it came free
When a buckle gave way – if that latter is true,
I much check for a bullet strike – I need a clue."

*"I believe that a bullet was meant for the King
But the Castle authorities won't stand a thing
Being said on the subject – they're standing aloof
And perhaps wouldn't budge even if shown the proof."*

He then listened to Holmes about someone called Mack
But when he heard 'Australian', was taken aback.
*"Mr Holmes, there's a man who, with fever, was shaken
And he's Antipodean, if I'm not mistaken."*

*"Australia, New Zealand – I just cannot say.
The accents I've heard are just far and away
Too alike for my ears to tell one from the other -
But they don't sound at all like your erudite brother."*

"Erudite?" Sherlock chuckled, *"He's flat on his back.
He may be well-schooled but the fellow does lack
Any empathy with those who don't wear a suit.
Now, what of that man of whom we're in pursuit?"*

*"He came looking for lodgings – I turned him away
Suggesting he find somewhere else he might stay.
With Victoria's funeral we're full to the brim
And we don't need disease brought here to us by him."*

*"Antipodean – well, that is interesting.
It's a lead, I admit - one worthy of testing
And chasing to ground. Do you know where he went?"*
Mused Sherlock, intrigued, *"We must be on his scent."*

"Well," Jenkins pondered, *"he wouldn't go far
He had trouble just leaning upon my front bar.
So I said he might try at St Marks for a bunk
They've a hostel for vagrants if they're not too drunk."*

152

"That occurred on the day the Queen's coffin rode by.
He came in after dark, I recall, and though try
As he might, I could offer no shelter that night
Even though he was ill, though he may have been tight."

"So you might try St Marks – he might be there or not.
It's the best I can do – it is all I have got."
Declared Jenkins with visions of impending doom.
"But, as for the harness, it's in the back room."

"Three patrons came in with the thing that same night
And explained where it came from and said with delight,
'We collected this harness – they threw it away.
We could sell for souvenirs, that's what they say'."

"It came off the Queen's carriage – the thing broke apart
So they cut the thing off so the sailors could start
Pulling just like the horses and move things along
So to grab it and sell it just couldn't be wrong."

Jenkins continued, *"Well I thought it might be*
Of some souvenir value to someone like me.
They were all on the slate for three modest amounts
So they gave the thing to me to square their accounts."

Sherlock, jumping about like a child with a toy,
Was finding it hard to contain his great joy
At receiving such clues when he thought he had failed.
"I declare that this night we might well have prevailed."

"Is the buckle still on it? I just need to check
Any signs of a bullet strike or any fleck
From a Leaden projectile which was left behind.
If I find it, I've proof but, if not, never mind."

"Yes, the buckle's attached but it won't be much good
As it's bent back and broken, that is understood.
Consider it your's, both the buckle and strap.
I hope you can make something of the mishap."

Sherlock looked at the buckle and promptly declared
It was bent by an impact not stretched out or flared
As it would be if put under excessive tension -
The search then took on a quite different dimension.

"I do not need a microscope or a Lead test
To declare that this buckle shows just the clearest
Signs of bullet strike – see the frame has been rent
And the bar and the prong ripped away as it bent."

"And the chape which attaches the buckle to strap
Is intact and not stretched – the harness didn't snap
But came suddenly loose causing great consternation
Then was cut and discarded, in my estimation."

"This news, straight to Major Wilkes, we must report
So he'll know we have evidence which will support
Suppositions we've made – an assassin's about
And the Castle's guards need to be on the lookout."

"We can only hope that the two monarchs will see
That there's danger for all, and that they will agree
To take greater precautions – their pride may result
In their deaths and, perhaps, even global tumult."

"So, if you've finished bleeding, Mycroft, then you ought
Go and see Major Wilkes and tell him you have brought
Him the proof that a shot had been fired toward
The cortège at an angle oblique and awkward."

"That, I'll do, Little Brother." said Mycroft, now pleased
That Big Henry had been, of his anger, appeased.
"Our carriage should be right out front, I expect,
And I'll take up that harness for Wilkes to inspect."

"But you'll have to be after that stalker of kings.
So, use all of your powers and do all those things
For which you are so famous – reach into that mind
Which is ultra-perceptive – this fiend, you must find."

Mycroft rolled up the harness and hurried outside
To the carriage there, waiting – at speed he would ride
To the Castle while Sherlock and Watson and Jakes
Went apace to St Marks for the two monarchs' sakes.

Jakes and Watson were armed, Sherlock counted on wits
And his knowledge of hand-to-hand combat where hits
Could be even more lethal than cudgels and clubs -
He may well have needed it searching those pubs.

THE VAGRANT

At St Marks vagrant hostel, a helper recalled
That a man with a fever was hostile and galled
Other helpers when told that he must sleep away
From the other men there if he wanted to stay.

The fever, they feared, might have spread to the rest
And they thought that to isolate him would be best.
"It was bitterly cold – he demanded a bunk
Near the fire, being sick, though he did appear drunk."

"We assigned him a bed in a separate room
Though he did make predictions of impending doom
If he wasn't kept warm – so more blankets we gave
To the fellow and told him he had to behave."

"He was gone in the morning, his blankets as well,
So the man is alive, as far as I can tell.
No one saw him arise, no one saw him depart,
And if you're looking for him, he's had a good start."

"Had he anything with him?" asked Sherlock, alert
To the great probability he was expert
In a number of deadly techniques and secreted
His weapons somewhere till his task was completed.

"I recall he came in without even a bag.
He was wearing a greatcoat and had an old rag
Wrapped right under his chin and up over each ear
Underneath a broad hat – his face wasn't so clear."

"Oh yes. Something else. Helpers tidied his room
And an object was struck by the side of a broom
Underneath the man's bed – so the helpers related -
A Laudanum bottle, quite empty, they stated."

"A Laudanum bottle! And it's empty you say?"
Cried out Watson, concerned that the man got away
But perhaps was unstable because of the drug.
"He might need to get more – his supply we must plug."

"Laudanum's not difficult to come by, My Friend,
And he may have lots more – we've no time to extend
Our search to suppliers of medical potions."
Said Sherlock, aware of two conflicting notions.

"A fever would lay the man low and prevent,
In all likelihood, any sound deployment
Of the tools of his trade – though if he's a fanatic
This fellow, if ailing, could just be erratic."

"If this fellow does fall into this category,
He may well decide that a great blaze of glory
Would sate his desire for mayhem and death -
All the more if approaching his terminal breath."

"But if he needs his drug for his hand to be steady
When poised to commit such a crime, then a ready
Supply of the stuff he'd have with him, I fear.
If that is the case, it and he are quite near."

"If the latter is true, we're obliged to assume
The assassination of the King will resume
Just as soon as the fellow can steady his nerve
And reach into that evil he keeps in reserve."

"I suggest that we search any buildings around
The vicinity of where that harness was found
To give way. We may find that a valuable clue
To the weapon remains in that deadly venue."

"You think such a man would leave something behind?"
Queried Jakes, *"It strikes me that he'd be of the kind*
Who would cover his tracks and leave nothing for those
Who were after him – although we do have your nose."

"My nose, I'll bring with me," Said Sherlock admitting
That clues might be wanting, *"and anything fitting*
The broadest description befitting a clue
I'll examine minutely – great effort is due."

"We must be off on foot for the carriage has taken
Mycroft to the Castle where he might awaken
The minds of the minders to danger extreme
For the royal cortège and those persons supreme."

"Four streets up, two across, and we'll be at the spot
Where the fellow we seek fired that errant shot.
The cortège headed off and the shot struck the left
Harness buckle and left us that tell-tale cleft."

"In the Station Concourse, I believe there occurred
With malicious intent, the event which had spurred
Into panic, the horses, although there have been
Quite divergent reports of what people had seen."

"We must search any building the Concourse is facing,
Opposite or attached, for it might help in tracing
The line of shot taken by this fellow 'Mack'.
With luck, it will help us go on the attack."

"We're working on guesswork – on getting untangled
The knot of conjecture on how the man angled
His gun to be fired to strike at the King
But missed when a horse shied and spoiled everything."

"Everything for the man, although not for the King
Nor for persons nearby who might have felt the sting
Of that bullet aimed right at the head of our nation,
Or perhaps someone else in that great congregation."

"It had come from the front – every clue coincides -
The King was protected on all other sides
And the Station was guarded by soldiers well-armed
To ensure that no one would, in transit, be harmed."

"Down the Concourse, it came, and the height, I suggest
Would at least be two storeys, so we'll have, at best,
Just three possible sites where the shot had been fired.
Let us hope we are led to the clue that's desired."

Access would be limited, that they all knew,
But they had to do something - their options were few
Though they might at least find the most probable site
Occupied by that fellow of devilish spite.

But some hours of searching and climbing drain pipes
Gave the trio no clue, though a series of gripes
Was heard coming from Watson supported by Jakes -
"We must discover something before the King wakes."

For the day was upon them, they'd not found a clue
To support the assertions which Holmes could construe
As a definite threat – he would have to act soon
Or the King might be dead by the same afternoon.

His hope was that Mycroft's report was persuasive.
With people below him, he could be abrasive
But carried authority of high degree
And, to use it with passion, the man could be free.

But, although the buckle and harness had shown
Evidence of a bullet strike, Mycroft had known
That, despite his authority covering most things,
He took orders, not gave them, when addressing Kings.

He'd harangued Major Wilkes and the royal retinue
And had shown everybody the ultimate clue
That a bullet was fired – the man did his best
But, in person, was told by the King, *"You're a pest."*

He could then only hope that the guards were alert
To a definite threat by an able expert
In the handling of small arms, the killing of men -
Mycroft said *"God help us!"* and Wilkes said *"Amen!"*

As dawn came upon them, all four felt defeat
Rising up all around them, and felt the great heat
Of determined exertion, in spite of the cold -
Disastrous events were about to unfold.

The day would be bitter, the Winter was bleak,
But the guards had been stirring, each man at the peak
Of his power and training – each knew an attempt
Might be made, so, from duty no one was exempt.

But another was stirring – he'd started to push
Off his thick wad of blankets – a perfect ambush
Had been planned in his mind, if not in great detail,
And he thought to himself *"If I miss, then I fail."*

He had slept under bushes, extensive and thick,
Near the road from the Castle – the fellow could stick
Close to ground, like the shadow he often had cast
On the African Veldt in his combative past.

He'd a vantage point, perfect, or so he had thought;
He'd give nobody quarter and none would be sought.
He'd beaten his fever but, to life, though he'd cling,
He'd be dead by that evening, but so would the King.

He had only to wait for he knew the parade
Of contemptible mourners, that heartless charade
Of pretenders in uniform, looking so fine,
Would all, out from the Castle, come marching in line.

He thought of the men he had killed in their names
Simply doing his duty in faraway games,
And his men who had died when the Boer fired back,
And of Glory and Gold and the Union Jack.

They'd remember that day when the war came to them
And remember the blood flow they tried hard to stem
As the King, the First Soldier, bled out on the ground
And the feeblest of heartbeats was not to be found.

In his mind, it was he whom the King had deserted,
The faraway soldier who'd simply inverted
The instincts and skills he had honed in the field -
He would strike at the Empire and would never yield.

Nought to gain, nought to lose – like an automaton
He would charge into battle and wave the baton
Of revenge at the ones who had brought his men off
With a medal, a trinket at which he would scoff.

Holmes, Watson and Jakes rejoined Mycroft who told
Them of warning the Castle but getting a cold
And quite hostile reception from those upon high
Even though he had proof an assassin was nigh.

*"There is no way they'll listen, though Wilkes did assist
By increasing the Guard, saying he would persist
With more stringent arrangements, as much as he could,
Though, to simply ignore him, he knew that they would."*

*"So we'll just have to find him ourselves, so prepare
To explore high and low for we just cannot dare
Risk this man being loose and preparing to kill
Either King or the Kaiser for revenge or thrill."*

"Sherlock, you know him and what he can do.
Well, a great deal more that the rest of us who
Have been trying to find him – your senses have shown
Us a man who'd have otherwise remained unknown."

"I can't take all the credit – Watson found him first."
Declared Sherlock, *"The man has a positive thirst*
For the truth, and for catching the felon red-handed.
Full credit to Watson, I'd say, was demanded."

"Well, don't go all mushy, there's credit aplenty.
I know for a fact that there are more than twenty
Who might claim a portion." said Watson, embarrassed.
"The important thing is to get McIntyre harassed."

"No! Gentlemen, please." Jakes then interrupted
"Enough of this drivel. We'd have him disrupted
If we had an inkling of what he was thinking
And also, perhaps, what he needs to be drinking."

"My experience tells me a Laudanum bottle
Suggests a weak man we might easily throttle.
It's a shame we've no time, for I'm sure we could plug
His supply and, so, cut the man off from his drug."

"I would flood the whole place with an ocean of Red
And string long lines of Blue so that if our man fled
Or might foolishly try to fulfil his desire,
He would fail and suffer a punishment dire."

Mycroft came in here saying, *"Wilkes said that he would*
Take it upon himself, at all places he could,
To have riflemen stationed at high elevation
In full sight of the killer to cause him vexation."

"Every soldier's post would be known to those sited
On either side of him – they'll get all excited
Should rifles project from where rifles should not,
In which case the owners would likely be shot."

"Well, at last here's some action." said Sherlock alert
To the merest response which might act to divert
More resources to guarding the cortège and King -
Still they were not prepared to prevent everything.

It seemed that the King and cortège would walk out,
Perhaps ride, as if daring assassins to sprout
From their hideaways, despite those efforts redoubled
By those who, for their safety, were very much troubled.

With guards in position and lookouts aloft,
Wilkes could only relate to a stymied Mycroft
That he'd like to have mobile troops mounted along
The itinerary taken – troops well-armed and strong.

"I have been over-ruled on that point, I regret,
But my orders are such that I'm able to let
Split detachments of troops first conduct what will be
Several sweeps of the route that will satisfy me."

"The last of the sweeps will be done out of sight
Of the King, just ahead of the cortège which might,
With good luck and good groundwork, not suffer attack.
We shall have to do likewise upon their way back."

Mycroft went on relating what Wilkes had arranged
And agreeing the Royal response was deranged,
But said also, right under that right Regal nose,
Sense prevailed and Wilkes had some more to propose.

"Wilkes said, though irregular in the extreme,
That we might care to join him - he has a supreme
Sense of duty and will have a few extra mounts
On the last of the sweeps – every extra eye counts."

"Watson held a commission and that helps a lot;
Jakes, a former detective well versed in the plot,
And Sherlock, my brother – I've vouched for you all.
As for me, I've been told to get back to Whitehall."

"The P.M. knows I'm missing – he's ordered me back
And I have to obey him – your options I lack.
'Get back to your office', the P.M. insists,
'That is, if you've damaged enough Windsor fists'."

"Ah! He knows of the blood that you shed in the quest
For our 'phantom assassin' – perhaps it is best
To return – you may help in the grim aftermath."
Said Sherlock, aware of officialdom's wrath.

"There will be repercussions, no matter how well
All our efforts together have acted to quell
The conspiracy made by those men who would bring,
To our shores, violence on our country and King."

"Should the King chance to fall to the stroke of the beast
All such efforts will not count towards us the least,
For we'll be the ones who had tried but had failed
And those who did nothing, we'll find, have prevailed."

"So, go back and write up a report stating all.
Should the King, on this day, be assailed and fall,
We'll need someone of power to stand up and say
That we all did our duty on this fateful day."

164

"I'll do that," Mycroft stated, *"but though I shed blood,*
I do fear, with the P.M., I'll swim in a flood
Of hot vitriol, verbal, for being away
From my post on our nation's most harrowing day."

"I'll just stand there and take it, I'll bow and I'll scrape.
But the P.M. does need me so I will escape
With a 'Your country needs you', 'You must be on call',
As I look past his shoulder and stare at the wall."

"Do your best to aid Wilkes – as a Major he fits
As man of some rank but he freely admits
He gets orders of which he might well disapprove,
He obeys, but sometimes there is some room to move."

"Remember the rules which bind him are severe.
When he asks you to help him, do not interfere
With his men or his planning – he'll stretch things as far
As he judges he's able – there's no one on par."

"Take your leave, Brother Mine, and be off to your post
And leave us here at ours – we'll be flushing this ghost
From his miserable haunts." Sherlock said, knowing well
That, for being away, Mycroft could receive Hell.

Mycroft rushed to the Station while Watson and Jakes
Joined Holmes in their carriage to do all it takes
To assist in the sweeps Major Wilkes organised -
With their help, his great efforts might be maximised.

165

THE SWEEPERS

McIntyre and Holmes, deadly rivals extreme
Had been bonded, somehow, in a perilous scheme
Which would have the King murdered or else kept alive.
Each determined the other was not to survive.

Sherlock had come to view this opponent not just
As a dangerous villain but someone who must
Be removed from the face of the Earth for all time
Lest he live and become the new Master of Crime.

Wilkes' sweeps of the route of the cortège well fitted
His view of the man against whom they were pitted.
He had to be swept from his vermin-filled nook
With a hard bristle broom – nothing less would he brook.

But he well knew his prey wouldn't just up and run
At the first sign of danger – he'd reach for his gun
Ever ready to fight to the death or he'd hide
To await what the Fortunes of Fate would provide.

He was wily and knew how to judge a position;
He had all of the attributes and intuition
Possessed by a predator stalking its prey -
Every possible line of attack he'd survey.

For as long as it took, he would stick to the ground
Never moving and inch, never making a sound,
Till the prey happened by, into range took a stride -
The time to attack would be his to decide.

But this prey wasn't something so simply confounded.
He was ever the dominant male surrounded
By lesser males sworn to protect and defend
Both the herd and its leader right up to the end.

The prey's swagger, however, displayed foolish pride
When it came to confronting danger from outside
And at distance - an attacker might strike and withdraw
And be gone before any could unsheathe a claw.

Foolish pride was, in fact, a deplorable trait,
A Heel of Achilles held bare to await
Any arrow or bullet, from near or afar,
A trait of his family - King, Kaiser or Czar.

The first sweep to be made started just on sunrise
As a mounted troop gathered intent to surprise
Anyone who had hidden by night to await
The cortège passing by at a good steady gait.

It would split into parties and double check any
Locations which might offer shelter, though many
Would not offer cover a killer would need
If he would, at his dastardly business, succeed.

With sabres held high, at thick bushes they'd rush,
Prodding madly and yelling so that they might flush
Anyone taking cover beneath for the night -
They would capture the killer or put him to flight.

All the way out to Frogmore, the mounted men kept
Up their frightening antics as onward they swept
The whole route and surrounds, clearing off anyone
Of suspicion – those men knew what was to be done.

The Frogmore Mausoleum where Albert had lain
Was awaiting Victoria so that, again,
Both together they could, for eternity, be
That couple She always referred to as 'We'.

But, despite protestations, Wilkes said that he must
Check the tomb and surroundings, respectfully, just
To make sure the assassin had not hid within -
The attendants acceded with mild chagrin.

He'd enter unarmed as a sign of respect
Hoping that, an armed killer, he would not detect.
His men were outside, everyone standing steady,
Their hands on their weapons, each man at the ready.

The first sweep yielded little of which to report,
Four fellows of quite an unsavoury sort -
Three vagrants and one rather miserable toff,
All drunken and sodden, just sleeping it off.

Having failed to make it to hostel or home,
Each had spent the night under the sheltering dome
Of a bush barely covered, its leaves mostly lost -
Discarded newspaper had kept off the frost.

But in parts, there were bushes with leaves still retained,
Mostly small, but some larger ones may have contained
An assassin in waiting – all had to be proved
To be empty or have any sleepers removed.

McIntyre, of course, had spent many a night
Under cold cloudless skies, all prepared for a fight
Covered only with blankets bespattered with grass
Stuck with mud while he waited for darkness to pass.

He would dig a low ditch and spread some of the spoil
On a water-soaked blanket beneath which he'd coil
After spreading it over with grass where he'd stay
Till the enemy came by or moved well away.

He would hide in plain sight of his foe who would see
Only grassy brown ground – so the man would be free
To emerge when he knew it was time to attack -
He'd remain undetected, this killer called Mack.

While awaiting the King, he would do just the same
As if after the Boer in the deadliest game
Played by one man alone using cunning and wits -
Such a man may well fail but that man never quits.

Just the odd sip of water, the odd bit of food,
And a mean disposition kept him in a mood
Of determined abhorrence of He that he's kill -
For hours on end he would have to keep still.

As a much fitter man he had done this before
When he felt quite invincible – most would deplore
Any thought of such hardship, but he was the one
Who would do what it takes to bring rivals undone.

Though his fever had broken, it might well return,
And his hiding place wasn't the right place to burn
And to shake as the soldiers were all going past -
He had Laudanum with him – he hoped it would last.

It was all that could help him when fever set in
But the stuff fed a demon just under his skin.
It would calm down that fever but often would light
Up a fire within him which he couldn't fight.

That demon within him demanded its due
And would torment his body and make him pursue
More and more of the Laudanum, dragging him deep
Into hellish oblivion, craving for sleep.

So, this man who stood tall found his limits and knew
He was held in the clutches of that evil brew.
Once he'd uncorked that bottle, the genies emerged
And, onto every nerve in his body, converged.

"If I have to go down," he so often had bragged,
"I'll take many more with me – I'll have the lot dragged
Down to Hades beside me, to eternal night,
And forever continue our eternal fight."

In his pit, he felt half-way to Hades already
But the demons were sated for now and a steady
Hand clutched his air-rifle, Moran's favourite toy -
Attacking in silence, Moran did enjoy.

Now that toy had passed on to a man on a quest,
A man full of hatred, a man who'd divest
Himself of any comfort in bringing the fight
To the foe, quite regardless of personal plight.

He heard all the yells of the soldiers who swept,
From the path of the cortège, the ones who had slept
Under bushes or bench, having nowhere to go -
All their curses rang out as a foul crescendo.

As the soldiers went past he remained undetected.
The ruse of the grass-covered blanket protected
This man in the ground from a full fifty pairs
Of eyes mounted up high on those soon to despair.

A quick look he chanced and he saw it was clear,
There were no mounted soldiers anywhere near.
He had hours to wait for the King to arrive -
He must keep very still if he'd hope to survive.

That the troops would return, he was certain, so he
Had to stick to his hideout - he just had to be
Like an unmoving stone for a few hours more
Then he would, by his reckoning, even the score.

His location was such that, the King, he could view;
It was right under bushes which had very few
Leaves to hide or give shelter to those who might stay;
For the soldiers, no one that they'd need move away.

Two hours went by and a second sweep came,
This time less intense as it covered the same
Terrain over which the same soldiers had ridden -
Complacency, though, was expressly forbidden.

"If it looks out of place, you should give it a prod
With the point of your sabres – you all have the nod
To be way over-zealous – no clue should be missed,
And no person, suspicious, just blithely dismissed."

McIntyre, peering out at this time, would observe
All the soldiers returning, a sight to unnerve
Any average person – something he was not -
He had to keep still or, his hideout, they'd spot.

One more swig of his Laudanum, that's what he'd need
Though he knew very well that he ought not exceed
What was needed to keep him from starting to shake,
Certainly not so much that he'd not stay awake.

He had slept through the night but, at dawn, was awake
At which time, food and water, in small lots he'd take;
He felt cramp coming on him – he needed to stretch
And unlike as a younger man, felt quite a wretch.

171

One limb at a time, he would lengthen full out
Till he felt somewhat better – he'd then heard the shout
Of the soldiers approaching – he had to keep still -
He reminded himself he'd a King he must kill.

Now they'd come back again just as if they knew where
He was hiding and waited to hear the shout *"There!"*
And the fall of the hooves of the horses and then
The sting of the sabres from all those King's men.

But the soldiers went by and could see nothing new,
Nothing suspicious had come into view.
The frost on the ground remained gray as before
And crunched with each footfall as, on, each horse bore.

Then nothing, not even a bird, could he hear;
Not even the fall of the snow on that clear
Dismal day – cold bit at him, he needed to move
But knew that, a fatal mistake, it might prove.

He would take just a little more food and then drink
Some more water, a sip, perhaps two, and then sink
Into mild discomfort and think on his quest -
One way or the other, when done, he would rest.

After hours, interminable, came the sound
Of the steady clip-clop of the horses all bound
For the Windsor Great Park, gun carriage in tow -
Victoria carried, respectfully slow.

"Now, a short swig or two of my foul Devil's Brew
Just to help clear my head as the King comes in view."
Mack said unto himself as he gingerly gazed
At a target at which even he was amazed.

In the distance, the King and the cortège progressed
But ahead of it, riding, was one who had messed
Up the empire of crime Moriarty assembled -
It was Holmes, or somebody he closely resembled.

The soldiers were, once again, sweeping the way
Of the solemn procession of those who'd display
Any possible threat – although loyal subjects
Were now milling in thousands to pay their respects.

It was too far to tell, but Mack fancied he saw
With an officer, mounted, three men who would draw
His attention by being civilians amid
A detachment of soldiers – something he'd forbid.

There were several detachments but most simply walked
Keeping pace with the cortège, this other one stalked
Like a predator seeking a fresh bloody kill -
Now he was the quarry – he'd have to keep still.

They avoided the crowds and looked at the terrain -
Any feature unusual, everything plain.
They seemed to be thoroughly searching as they
Approached closer and closer to their hidden prey.

Though he only had seen Sherlock's picture, he knew
That it was the Great Meddler, toward him, who drew
Ever closer, each minute – he might chance a shot
At that deerstalkered menace but, then, perhaps not.

A wounded or dead Sherlock Holmes would alert
The entire contingent that someone expert
In small arms, an assassin, was somewhere about,
Then *"Protect the King"* would go up with a shout.

The cortège would be halted, surrounded by troops;
Mounted soldiers would gallop in hostile swoops
Of the country around where the Great Meddler fell -
What they'd do if they found him, Mack knew very well.

It would not be a soldierly shot to the head,
He'd be hacked down by sabres, lucky to be dead
But more likely to linger in terrible pain -
The King would live on and, so, Mack would refrain.

One civilian, he felt, would be Watson, however
The other civilian was someone he never
Laid eyes on before, not in photo or flesh,
Just one more complication, an obstacle fresh.

Sherlock Holmes was a prize of much smaller degree
Than the King was to be – he would need to stay free
Till they galloped away having found not a thing
If he was to lay claim to that trophy, the King.

Some minutes went by and heard horses moving
Away from his hideout, distinctly improving
His chance of a shot at the King when he came
Into view and to range – so much for the Sleuth's fame.

But he had to keep still for a few minutes more
In case Holmes was on foot. Being cramped to the core
He was finding it hard not to stretch out a leg -
For a minute of movement, to Hades, he'd beg.

That minute was granted when no one appeared
And it seemed that a path to the King had been cleared.
But this line of sight offered would not last for long
As the guard gathered in, ever-ready and strong.

With the air-gun prepared and the King now in sight
McIntyre experienced tremendous delight
But could not get his aim through the gathering guard.
He could not risk a shot – this was proving too hard.

Only one chance remained for a shot at the King.
He must wait, once again, for the cortège to swing
Past the very same spot, although this time at pace
As it, back to the Castle, its tracks, would retrace.

The soldiers were tired, likewise every guard.
They had seen not one threat, not a single small shard
Of support for assassins being lurking about.
Wilkes felt like he'd suffered a ruinous rout.

With darkness impinging, Mack watched the approach
Of the King sitting high in the grand Royal Coach
And he crept from his hideout and slowly took aim -
This greatest of trophies was now his to claim.

At that moment an alert Sherlock Holmes gave a yell,
Major Wilkes made a prearranged sign to compel
The King's Coach to take action and swerve well away
From what might be a threat or at least an affray.

Sherlock Holmes had seen only what he took to be
A quite suspicious movement, a movement that he
Had envisaged as someone who'd run out and crouched
But, if it was the killer, he could not have vouched.

As the soldiers spread out looking for any sign
Of whoever Holmes saw, a vague figure, malign
Had been spotted by one who spurred forward apace,
His sabre aloft and resolve on his face.

Mack saw the man coming and fired one shot.
No one heard any sound but he clearly had got
His opponent, oncoming – the man hit the ground,
A dent in his helmet, his head spinning 'round.

Mack, ever the man of great exploits, took hold
Of the reins of the horse, jumping on with a bold
Single action and rode like a demon away -
He had failed – he would try again some other day.

THE SPOILS

Just a horse - it was something, it put space between
McIntyre and death, for the others had seen
The man jump to the saddle and gallop at speed -
Night had fallen – to get to some shelter he'd need.

He had no time stop, not a chance for a shot.
For a minute or two McIntyre forgot
About Gold, Moriarty, Moran and the King -
To the horse and its reins, to survive, he must cling.

It was darkening quickly, long shadows had formed,
But behind closing swiftly were three uniformed
Horsemen riding at pace, sabres ready to hack
At the flesh of the man who had made the attack.

There'd be no quarter given if he would be caught
For, one thing that his days in South Africa taught
Was that, if blood was rushing and tempers were hot,
Compassion and mercy most fighters forgot.

One caught up with Mack and he took a wild swing
Hoping that, with one blow, he'd be able to bring
His man down – he connected, he'd struck the air-gun
But he did hear a yell from this man on the run.

He was slashed on the shoulder, the gun took the brunt
Of the blow - if it hadn't, the desperate hunt
Would have ended right there but he wasn't dead yet -
He'd show them he was the best fighter they'd met.

Through town, past the station, toward Windsor Bridge,
With his blood seeping out from a gash on the ridge
Of his shoulder, he rode through the wagons and drays
Getting loads from the railway and going their ways.

The same mounted soldier came on him once more,
From the opposite side - McIntyre just swore
In a rage, *"You'll not take me."* then swung at the head
Of the man with his air-gun – he went down like Lead.

But the air-gun went with him and Mack cursed aloud
And he wondered if this was the end of a proud
And distinguished career, both of soldiering and crime -
There were things left do if he just had the time.

But to stop, he had no time, none even to slow.
He could now see the water ahead in the glow
Of the yet-to-rise moon – he would have to be quick
So he gave to his horse, with his boot, a last kick.

Then, onward he sped, to the Thames and a boat
Hoping that he'd be able to push off and float
Well away from the men who were riding up fast -
He would then disappear on that waterway, vast.

Several launches at moorings showed no sign of steam
And were too big to push to the slow moving stream.
He then noticed a dinghy held fast by a rope –
He'd jump in and he'd row and, to Hades, he'd hope.

With his shoulder gashed badly and blood oozing out,
He could not row effectively, splashing about,
But the river was dark and he just had to get
Far enough from the soldiers and then he'd be set.

The two soldiers who followed charged onward apace.
They were followed by Wilkes and his men in a race
To head off the assassin before he could flee
To the river and safety, somewhere he'd be free.

Holmes and Watson had followed as best as they could
But the Doctor had stopped just to see if he could
Be of help to the soldier who fell to the ground -
He had lesions and cuts and they had to be bound.

Sherlock Holmes had, however, rode on till he met
Up with Wilkes and his men. They were starting to get
Information from onlookers of someone who ran
And jumped into a boat like some crazy madman.

With the aid of the very faint moonlight they picked
Out his shape in the distance – the hammers were clicked
On revolvers which fired repeatedly at
The escaping assassin, now laying quite flat.

Now the moon, getting higher, provided more light
And the group on the shore said that one of them might
Well have struck him – Mack suddenly rose and then fell
But, if had been wounded, they just couldn't tell.

When the men had reloaded, they started anew
Firing madly toward him, the Lead that they threw
Could have sunk the boat several times over, but no
One could tell of the fate of its human cargo.

All at once, Mack arose with defeat on his face
But he would not submit, that would be a disgrace.
On the stern of the boat for a second he propped
And then, into the Thames to evade them, he dropped.

Several days saw the banks of the Thames all alive
With the movement of searchers. Could any survive
A deep cut on his shoulder and water so cold?
No one ever could – that's what Wilkes had been told.

The King wasn't convinced that there had been a plot
And refused, resolutely, to hear that a shot
Had been fired: *"An air-gun! That's only a toy
And not what a decent marksman would employ."*

He went off, the next morning, to places unknown
Thinking that the whole matter had been overblown
Leaving Wilkes looking foolish to those who were not
There to witness the thwarting of McIntyre's plot.

"Such is life in the Army." said Wilkes with a grin,
*"But I know what we did – we must lose or must win
As the war gods decide. We are soldiers, you know,
We obey all our orders and go with the flow."*

Two days later, a meeting with Mycroft revealed
That the entire matter, for now, had been sealed
On the orders of someone who need not be named -
He would not have a tense situation inflamed.

Mycroft said, "*Brother Mine, leave such matter behind*
And seek mysteries of a less sensitive kind.
We shall never know all of the facts of this case -
There are many more felons which we'll have to chase."

"*I say 'We', I mean 'You' and your medical friend,*
So accept that this matter is now at an end.
It has passed from this office to chambers beyond
My domain and control – they will never respond."

Sherlock nodded agreement but said, "*May I ask?*
Sir Humphrey went west on some unknown task.
Was this somehow related to recent events?
During our recent hunt we lost several scents."

"*Well, it was, in a way,*" Mycroft said in reply,
"*Though I am not permitted to give you the why*
And the wherefore about where and what he had done
Though I can say his efforts were second to none."

"*Thank you, Brother Mycroft, I've learned not a thing*
But I must say it has a familiar ring."
Replied Sherlock, "*I do suppose Windsor is west.*
Perhaps he was waiting to meet a new guest?"

"*Perhaps!*" declared Mycroft, "*such things are arranged*
In advance, but I'll tell you arrangements have changed.
You must tell Dr Watson to lay down his pen -
For the moment write nothing, I'll let you know when."

Holmes and Watson met up at the Baker Street lair,
Watson saying, "*The whole thing is just so unfair.*
I have reams of blank paper awaiting a nib
Charged with ink. Does he think I would utter a fib?"

"Against Whitehall and Windsor, I'd not like to go,
So if Mycroft gives to you a definite 'No'
I would say he's been told by the highest there is."
Sherlock warned, *"And you know the decision's not his."*

"So, let sleeping dogs lie – they are best left alone
And do not test them out with a succulent bone
For they do have a bite which is worse than their bark
And you could come to grief for the slightest remark."

"They want this thing over – we must let it be
And for now be content with the knowledge that we
Have just thwarted the last of the menacing men
Moriarty assembled – his evil brethren."

"To the victors, the spoils; the vanquished have gone
And I'd say that a brighter light never has shone
On our land as it does on this wintery day -
Let us hope that its brightness, forever, will stay."

Watson nodded approval and, so, had agreed
That some facts must stay secret – he did see the need
For restraint and discretion in all that he wrote
Although he was keen for at least one anecdote.

So, he then put away, for the present at least,
All the notes he had made of that 'damnable beast
From the Veldt' who craved Gold for the power it brings
While decrying that power invested in Kings.

But, again, the vile powers of evil had failed
When, by being alert, its opponents prevailed
Having taken the challenge, the sword and the lance
And had been, into battle, prepared to advance.

So that problem was gone and with it the danger
Of violent change to a world so much stranger.
Watson pondered the evils which they'd been taxed
As a reflective Sherlock Holmes lyrically waxed.

Pipe in hand, looking out over Baker Street's hustle,
He found reassurance in all of its bustle,
Its flurry of feet as they stepped on their ways
And he thought, *"We are now in for much better days."*

"Looking over this city, the life I behold,
Though it's so often measured in ounces of Gold,
It the stuff of Great Britain – it's not just in Kings
But in honest folk doing their everyday things."

"You and I, we are guardians, in our own way,
Of those small honest folk who go on, day by day,
In this city of millions doing work, cheek by jowl,
Unaware of the jackals and wolves on the prowl."

"These past days we have thwarted the last of a gang
Who, if he had been caught, would assuredly hang.
But he's now joined those other two felons supreme
In the ashes and rubble of their evil scheme."

"McIntyre, Moran, Moriarty – they're gone.
On this Earth, I declare, that the light never shone
On a more evil trio than those who had hatched
A foul plot for a conflict with death-toll unmatched."

"The deceit, the depravity – can we not see
That the world is improved by the absence of three
Most despicable people that ever drew breath?
I, myself, find it hard not to cheer at each death."

"McIntyre almost brought off the foulest of crimes
But was beaten by forces which, in these strange times
Were alert to the evil which triumphs unless
We take action together to thwart its success."

"He's the worst of the trio, is some ways, at least;
He had all of those attributes born of The Beast;
Moriarty - deluded; Moran had gone mad;
But this Menace from Melbourne was totally bad."

"I do hope, in the future, good sense will prevail
And the young men of Europe will never assail
One another in combat – there's too much at stake
There is much to achieve if, the right course, we take."

"So I pray our new King will be able to bring
A new sense of commitment to peace heralding,
For all Europe, and also the world, a fresh start
In our dealings and keep our great armies apart."

"I have hopes, also, Watson, this land can improve
The sad lot of so many who just cannot move
From their lives in our slums, the abyss from which few
Can see past lives of crime to a much brighter view."

"Our Empire is changing, becoming mature
As Dominions develop and firmly ensure
That our civilisation will prosper and grow -
From colonies, many new nations will flow."

"The Dominion of Canada started this move
And those lands, Australasian, I'm certain will prove
To be nations united by kinship and creed
Though a few rotten apples will succumb to greed."

"But I know, by and large, they are excellent sorts
In those faraway lands which have, by all reports,
Accepted all challenges, day by hard day,
And a movement to greatness is well underway."

"Melbourne's risen up high from Australia's hard soil
But, while most are no strangers to hard honest toil,
Such a place will attract both the felon and cheat
And there'll always be evil to thwart and to beat."

"But our people are up to the challenge, I know,
And our civilisation is destined to grow
To a greatness unknown since all time had begun
And, the shadows of evil, our people will shun."

"So, a toast to our world-wide Empire, I say,
For we've foiled the plot which, in our present day,
Posed a far greater threat than we'd met in the past
And that Menace from Melbourne, we're free of at last."

Watson pondered this statement. The man did agree
With its sentiments, surely, but Mack did jump free.
He'd prefer to have stopped him with bullet or rope
So said under his breath, *"My Dear Friend, I do hope!"*

****

184

Sherlock Holmes and The Menacing Moors

A call from an old comrade has Holmes chasing a reported agent of Satan between the towering tors and bottomless bogs of Dartmoor only to find the limits of his own confidence and his Public's esteem. Only Watson stands his friend but even his patience is stretched. Sherlock's retreat to the bees of Sussex serves only to show him that his skills are unique and are desperately needed elsewhere. On returning to London, Holmes finds malign forces have been bringing ridicule to his doorstep. In this tale, the Great Sleuth is brought to life, uniquely, in expressive verse, a favourite form of the author who loves the language of Sherlock Holmes and the Menacing Moors.

Also from Allan Mitchell

Sherlock Holmes and The Menacing Metropolis

More Menacing than the Menacing Moors, the Great Metropolis harbours evil and deviltry far more sinister than Dartmoor could offer - it is not for nothing that Watson describes London as the great cesspool draining the Empire of its dregs. Its evil stems from the hearts of the most heartless of men, evil against which a group of stalwart Londoners is determined to act. Knowledge is power and forewarned is forearmed, it is said, but fore-knowledge is fragile and Sherlock must balance probability with instinct, caution with decisiveness, when warned of impending disaster for both City and Realm. Allan Mitchell's stirring stanzas of reeling rhyme once again stretch back to an earlier era to witness the never-ending battle between Sherlock Holmes and the Menacing Metropolis.

Also from MX Publishing

MX Publishing is the world's largest specialist Sherlock Holmes publisher, with over a hundred titles and fifty authors creating the latest in Sherlock Holmes fiction and non-fiction.

From traditional short stories and novels to travel guides and quiz books, MX Publishing cater for all Holmes fans.

The collection includes leading titles such as _Benedict Cumberbatch In Transition_ and _The Norwood Author_ which won the 2011 Howlett Award (Sherlock Holmes Book of the Year).

MX Publishing also has one of the largest communities of Holmes fans on Facebook with regular contributions from dozens of authors.

www.mxpublishing.com

Also from MX Publishing

Our bestselling short story collections 'Lost Stories of Sherlock Holmes', 'The Outstanding Mysteries of Sherlock Holmes', 'Untold Adventures of Sherlock Holmes' (and the sequel 'Studies in Legacy') and 'Sherlock Holmes in Pursuit'.

www.mxpublishing.com

London, 1920: Boston-bred Enoch Hale, working as a reporter for the Central Press Syndicate, arrives on the scene shortly after a music hall escape artist is found hanging from the ceiling in his dressing room. What at first appears to be a suicide turns out to be murder . . .

(the first in the Sherlock Holmes and Enoch Hale trilogy)

www.mxpublishing.com

Also from MX Publishing

Sherlock Holmes Re-Imagined

Twelve original adventures from Sir Arthur Conan Doyle,
re-illustrated in Lego.

In this book series, the short stories comprising The Adventures of Sherlock Holmes have been amusingly illustrated using only Lego® brand minifigures and bricks. The illustrations recreate, through custom designed Lego models, the composition of the black and white drawings by Sidney Paget that accompanied the original publication of these adventures appearing in The Strand Magazine from July 1891 to June 1892.

www.mxpublishing.com

Also from MX Publishing

"Phil Growick's, 'The Secret Journal of Dr Watson', is an adventure which takes place in the latter part of Holmes and Watson's lives. They are entrusted by HM Government (although not officially) and the King no less to undertake a rescue mission to save the Romanovs, Russia's Royal family from a grisly end at the hand of the Bolsheviks. There is a wealth of detail in the story but not so much as would detract us from the enjoyment of the story. Espionage, counter-espionage, the ace of spies himself, double-agents, double-crossers...all these flit across the pages in a realistic and exciting way. All the characters are extremely well-drawn and Mr Growick, most importantly, does not falter with a very good ear for Holmesian dialogue indeed. Highly recommended. A five-star effort."
The Baker Street Society

www.mxpublishing.com

www.ingramcontent.com/pod-product-compliance
Lightning Source LLC
Chambersburg PA
CBHW051511170626
46811CB00002B/767